THE NORTHWEST COUNTRY

THE NORTHWEST COUNTRY

A novel of the American frontier

JEFFERSON FLANDERS

Munroe Hill Press
Lexington, Massachusetts

Cover design by Mick Wieland Design

ISBN: 0-9908675-3-6
ISBN-13: 978-0-9908675-3-1
eBook ISBN: 978-0-9908675-4-8

Munroe Hill Press
Lexington, Massachusetts

For Stephen Carver Flanders, a storyteller who loved his country and its history

Remember that you are an actor in a play the character of which is determined by the Playwright; if He wishes the play to be short, then it is short; if long, it is long. If He wishes you to play the part of a beggar, remember to act even this role adroitly; and so if your role be that of a cripple, an official, or a layman. For this is your business, to play admirably the role assigned you; but the selection of that role is Another's.

– Epictetus, *The Enchiridion*

A HISTORICAL NOTE

Liberty. Equality. Independence. Those principles—boldly advanced by American revolutionaries in the 1760s and 1770s—in turn helped inspire global political ferment, including the French revolution in 1789; a slave revolt in Saint-Domingue beginning in 1792; an uprising against British rule of Ireland in 1798; and growing calls in England and the United States for the abolition of chattel slavery.

The founders of the new American Republic, men of the Enlightenment, recognized the contradiction between their lofty calls for the rights of men and the realities of slavery. Yet in the South, slave labor produced the lucrative cash crops of tobacco and rice, and its immediate abolition would have had serious economic consequences for Southern elites. The leaders of the early Republic struggled with the correct course of action.

In 1787, the Congress of the Confederation established the Northwest Territory from lands west of the Appalachian Mountains, north of the Ohio River, and east of the Mississippi River. Slavery was prohibited in this vast new territory. In effect, the Ohio River became the natural boundary between slavery and freedom in the frontier lands of the Old Northwest. A clause in the enabling Northwest Ordinance promised the return of slaves who escaped across the river to their owners.

At the Constitutional Convention in the summer of 1797, Northern delegates eager to keep the new nation intact and avoid regional strife agreed to several compromises on slavery. The new Constitution gave Congress the authority to prohibit the importation of slaves after twenty years. For determining taxation and representation, slaves were counted as three-fifths of "free persons." A fugitive slave clause allowed the recovery of escaped slaves across state borders.

By the 1790s, the New England states (Vermont, Massachusetts, New

Hampshire, Connecticut and Rhode Island) and Pennsylvania had emancipated their slaves (in most cases gradually) and banned the institution. New York and New Jersey continued to allow slavery, and it had spread to the new states of Kentucky and Tennessee.

In 1793, Congress passed the Fugitive Slave Act, which allowed owners to seize escaped slaves—even in states that prohibited slavery. It also established penalties for obstructing efforts to recapture fugitive slaves, or for rescuing, harboring, or concealing them.

The Act encouraged slave catchers to capture and return many slaves to their owners, typically for a bounty. In some cases, free blacks were kidnapped by these bounty hunters and sold into slavery.

Those white settlers who sought to keep slavery from the Northwest Territory did so for differing reasons. Some wanted the West reserved only for whites (objecting to the introduction of freed blacks into Ohio and Illinois, as well). Others feared that free labor couldn't compete with slave labor. Many Quakers, Methodists, and other believers opposed slavery on religious grounds.

There were a few settlers north of the Ohio River who helped slaves on the run. They did so knowing that they were breaking the law, and that they risked violent clashes with the slave catchers sent into the Northwest country.

PART ONE

ONE

Kentucky, Summer 1798

The forest envelops them with an indifferent, uncaring stillness.

They move quickly along the abandoned Shawnee trace. There are five men and a young girl in the group headed toward the river, following the pathway northwest through the Kentucky hill country. They move single file, with a bearded, silver-haired man in the lead.

The only sounds are those of their labored breathing, the crackling of twigs and leaves under their feet, and the occasional rustling of a squirrel or chipmunk or other forest animal startled by their passage.

While is it only late afternoon, little sunlight penetrates the broad green canopy of trees above them, the buttonwoods, black walnuts, hickories, red maples, and oaks. The air remains warm and still, unmoved by breezes. Small pine trees, hanging wild grape vines, and dense, thick underbrush flank both sides of the trace.

The leader of this small group is an old man with a hard, unyielding face. His silver shock of hair and long beard set off his piercing blue eyes. He moves well for a man his age, striding up the path with determination.

His eyes constantly scan the forest before them, glancing side-to-side, alert for danger. Relative safety awaits on the other side of the river, in the land marked on the maps as the Northwest Territory. But for now, they are still in Kentucky and can expect no quarter if their pursuers catch up to them.

Just behind him, following, comes a black man, poorly dressed in a tattered shirt and trousers. He carries a small burlap bag and is barefoot.

Further down the trail, the girl rides piggyback on the broad back and shoulders of another black man, sturdily-built, whose coarse linen shirt is stained with sweat in the warm August air. There is an ugly scar, a brand in the shape of a "T" on the man's right cheek. His shoes are too large for his feet, and he struggles to avoid slipping on the occasional rocks scattered along the trace.

The girl's light amber face is exquisite—an exotic blending of African and European features. She wears a dirty cotton dress and a forlorn blue ribbon in her hair. She could be anywhere from twelve to sixteen years in age. She has closed her eyes and clings to the back of her ride with little strength; without his firm grasp on her legs, the constant jarring of his stride would topple her from her perch. Yet, he is a strong man, and shows little signs of tiring.

The last two men in the party follow some one hundred yards behind. They both wear deerskin hunting shirts, breeches, and moccasins, and they carry long rifles. One is tall with brown hair and hooded gray-blue eyes. The other man is slight of build, with dark hair and an olive complexion.

The brown-haired man stops occasionally and waits by the side of the trail, standing behind the trunk of one of the massive trees, waiting, listening intently, straining to catch the sounds of any pursuit. He has his rifle at the ready, but hears nothing to alarm him.

When the trail turns due west, the bearded man in the lead stops for a moment. He holds his hand up to stop the others behind him. He peers ahead into the forest, conscious of something. He slowly brings the rifle to his shoulder and cocks the hammer.

He waits, listening intently, straining to hear. There is nothing. Silence. The bearded man shakes his head. Perhaps they have surprised a fox or a wolf? He is not sure. Whatever has caused the movement, whatever he may have seen, it is not visible now.

He turns around, about to say something to his companions, when there is a sudden report from the stand of trees ahead of them. A bullet slaps into the bark of a nearby tree. Smoke rises in the air. The older man dives into the shelter of the forest. Moments later there is another report, and this time a hissing sound, and then a thud. The second man in line, the black man, emits a strange, keening sigh and collapses to the ground. The scarred man carrying the girl on his back seeks shelter on the other side of the trail.

There is no sign of the last two men in the party—they may have heard the gunshots and stopped—or they may have already melted into the dense, surrounding forest.

The only sound now is the moaning of the wounded black man. Then a deep and husky male voice calls out from somewhere ahead. "Leave the niggers. You cain't git away otherwises. Leave 'em and we'll let you be."

The wounded man cries out loudly in pain and confusion, and then is silent.

The bearded man crouches down behind the trunk of a large pine tree. He looks down at the pine needles on the ground under him and wonders if he will survive the day. He whispers a brief prayer.

Then he abandons the safety of the tree and crawls on his hands and knees to the wounded man. He places his hand on the man's throat to feel for a pulse—it takes only a few moments to realize that he is beyond help.

The bearded man suddenly rises to his feet and dashes across to join the girl and man huddled at the base of a large oak. His move provokes rifle fire, and several bullets clip off the leaves and trees around him, but the volley misses, and he reaches his destination unscathed.

"What 'bout Pompey?" the black man with the scar on his cheek asks.

"He has gone to the Lord."

The girl's eyes are wide with fear; she hugs her arms around her knees. She begins humming a tune, softly, trying to calm herself. Her looks are even more striking, the bearded man thinks, when her face is animated by strong emotion, as it is now.

"Cain't go back," the scarred man says. "Massa George kill me. He never hurt Flavia, but he kill me."

"There will be no going back, Cicero," the older man says.

"How dey know we gwin' be here, Mista Flint?" he asks.

"I don't know. There must be another trail to let them catch up to us. That's the only explanation that makes sense. No matter. Have faith. 'In thee O Lord do I put my trust: let me never be put to confusion.'"

"I try, Mista Flint, I try."

They are interrupted by another shout. "You git one more chance," the man yells. "Send the girl up the trail to us now, and Mr. Todd says you can go. You can keep the other nigger, he don't matter."

Flint shakes his head. He raises himself slightly and responds. "Why should we believe you?"

Another voice, higher-pitched and with a distinct Virginia accent, answers. "Simple enough. You have my word as a gentleman that if you return Flavia to me, now, we will allow you to depart in peace. Cicero may also leave. Be reasonable, sir. Would you place the girl in harm's way? If we must come to get her, there may be further violence. I only wish what is mine to be restored to me."

"Thas' Massa George," Cicero says. "Thas' his voice."

The girl Flavia shakes her head vigorously and whispers the word "no" three times. Flint strokes his beard nervously.

"We won't let any harm come to ye," Flint says to the girl, bending over so he can look into her face. "We won't let him have ye. Ye have the word of Daniel Flint on that."

He stands up, shielded by the tree, and calls back. "For they know not to do right, who store up violence and robbery in their palaces."

"Spout the Bible all afternoon, but you won't be leaving without my by-your-leave." The higher-pitched voice Cicero has identified as that of Master George is confident, assured, the voice of a man used to getting his way. "We can resolve this in short order. Send the girl to me now. You have taken her illegally. You have ten minutes. Or if you don't, I'll be forced to take stronger measures."

Flint does not reply. He has folded his hands together and has begun to pray. The man and girl watch him.

From up the trail, there is the sudden distant report of a rifle, then another, then a high piercing Indian war cry and the frantic shouts of men. Flint looks at the girl, Flavia, and then at Cicero with his fierce blue eyes and they stare back at him, unsure what is transpiring in the forest ahead of them.

They hear a voice, again in the distance, yelling: "Behind us, watch behind!" Another rifle is fired, then the sounds of men running through the forest in panic, of branches breaking. They hear men yelling indistinctly, their voices panicky and unsure.

Flint nods in satisfaction. "Judah and his friend must have caught Todd and his men unawares," he says.

The sounds become more distant and then subside. The forest reverts to its natural stillness. They wait in silence behind the tree. The girl has closed her eyes and continues to softly hum her song.

Five minutes later a voice calls out from the forest in front of them. "Flint? Cicero? It's Judah. Don't fire on us. We're coming back down the trail towards you."

"I hear ye. We'll hold fire."

Two figures appear: the tall, dark-haired man and his slighter companion. They carry tomahawks in their right hands and grip their flintlock rifles in their left.

Flint steps out into the trace to welcome them. "Praise God," he says. "Ye have delivered us from the evil-doers."

The tall man responds with disgust; he shakes his head angrily. "You said that no one would follow us. You promised no blood would be shed."

"Didn't we free the girl and Cicero without violence?" Flint asks. "Just as Pompey told us we could. How could we know that Todd and his men would follow us this far? We must praise God that you were here to smite down our enemies. You were God sent, Barnabas."

"I'm here only because I agreed to help out Judah," the man replies, with some bitterness. "Not to kill. Certainly not like this."

"What happened?" Flint asks Judah.

"There were six or seven of them," Judah says. He speaks with a slight French accent. "I don't know how they managed to get in front of us. They must have figured out our route."

"We knew that the girl would slow us down," Flint says. "It was a chance we had to take. At least you were able to surprise them."

"We circled their flanks after we heard the first shots," Judah says. "Came up on them from behind. We may have killed one of them." He pauses, uncertain. "A shot from Barnabas, actually. I may have winged another man when they fled."

Barnabas says nothing. Still angry, he glares at Flint, who looks back at him calmly.

"Six men, ye say," Flint replies. "If ye got one, then they're down to five."

"They have scattered for now," Barnabas says. "We should not tarry here for long."

"We lost Pompey in the ambush," Flint says. "A bullet in the chest. Cicero and Flavia are unharmed. We won't have time to properly bury Pompey. We must make for the river, cross before nightfall."

"There will be a bill come due for today's handiwork, Flint," Barnabas says. He is trying unsuccessfully to hold his anger in check. "There's a dead man in the woods."

Flint shakes his head. "Fear not. 'And mine eye shall not spare, neither will I have pity; I will recompense thee according to thine abominations that are in the midst of thee; and ye shall know that I am the Lord that smiteth.' These men were evil-doers. The Lord shall watch over us. We are in the right."

"Nonetheless, Barnabas is correct," Judah says quickly. "If we are caught on this side of the river we'll hang for murder, to say nothing of the charges for stealing Flavia and Pompey."

"Have we stolen them?" the older man asks. "In the eyes of the Lord? Or have we liberated those in bondage? That men who follow evil reap the whirlwind should come as no surprise. It's God's will."

Barnabas laughs harshly. "You'd argue with Satan himself, old man, and no doubt you'd prevail."

"Do ye not loathe the abomination of slavery?"

"It ain't right for one man to own another. I grant you that. I don't think you can single-handedly free every damn slave in Kentucky."

"We do what we can," Flint says. "Now we must return to Canaan as swiftly as we can."

"To Canaan, then," Judah says.

"Mark my words," Barnabas says. "It will not end here. A man has been killed."

"Two men," Flint says sternly. "Pompey is a man in the eyes of the Lord even if he comes from the lineage of Cain, the house of Ham."

"Two men are dead," Barnabas says, conceding the point. "Todd will be searching for the girl, asking questions on both sides of the river. If we bring her to Canaan, word will get out. Sooner or later, Todd and his men will come."

"We shall be ready, should that come to pass. God will watch over us."

Barnabas shakes his head, unconvinced. "This course is mistaken." He looks over at the girl. "You must find another place for her."

Flint stares at him, his chin thrust forward stubbornly. "I gave her, and her brother, my word. They will make their home with us. They will be safe in Canaan."

Judah shakes his head. "Is that wise? I agree with Barnabas, this man Todd won't let it go. He'll come after us. Would you place Rachel and Naomi at risk? Your own daughter and granddaughter?"

"Who isn't in danger? Satan and his allies never cease in their pursuit of the righteous."

"I'll stay with you in Canaan for a while," Barnabas says to Judah. "We'll need to keep our rifles handy and an eye out for Todd and his men. But I'd advise you to take your family and leave with me when the time comes."

"And when will that be?" Judah asks.

Barnabas looks past him down the trace to the country behind them. "Sooner rather than later. You can depend on that."

TWO

New York, Fall 1798

Calvin Tarkington had reached one of his favorite passages in his battered, leather-bound copy of the *Odyssey*, the verses where Penelope offers the ragged beggar she suspects might be her long-absent husband Odysseus a chance to string the King of Ithaca's great backstrung bow. As Calvin read the Greek a second time, admiring Homer's vivid imagery, there was a light rapping on the study door. A moment later, Livingston Rhodes poked his head inside.

"May I interrupt?" Rhodes asked, entering the study before Calvin had a chance to respond. "Good afternoon, Calvin."

"Good afternoon," Calvin replied. "What brings you to Greenwich Street, Livingston?"

"I've heard the news from Jean Laurent," Rhodes said, breathlessly, his face flushed with excitement. "It's true, is it? Abigail is leaving for Philadelphia."

"That she is," Calvin said, gazing up from the page, mildly annoyed by the interruption but still pleased to see his friend. "Her daughter had twins, and she's needed. Abigail's certainly more in demand there than she is here."

Abigail Soule had served faithfully as Calvin's housekeeper and cook for the last four years, ever since he decided to settle in Manhattan after concluding a highly profitable voyage to China. Calvin had purchased a sturdy and handsome brick house on Greenwich Street and relocated the shipping offices of Tarkington & Scott from his native Boston to the New York waterfront.

"What do you plan to do, then? About her departure?" Rhodes asked.

"It hardly ranks as a crisis in my book," Calvin said. "I'll simply take more of my meals at Fraunces Tavern. Jean will find someone to come in and clean and do the laundry."

Rhodes gave him a look of dismay. The sunlight streaming through the windows of the study reflected off his eyeglasses. "You'll be down to skin and bones in no time, without someone cooking for you. I know that you'll skip meals. Mrs. Soule kept a close eye on that."

"Did she?"

"And she was diligent in making sure that the house remained clean and fit for entertaining," Rhodes said. "As befits someone of your station."

"My station?" Calvin grinned. "That doesn't sound like a concern for a dedicated republican. What would your readers at the *New York Gazette* think? You're not becoming a Federalist in your old age, are you? Worried about my station? Is this a sea change in your political loyalties?"

Livingston responded calmly to his friend's teasing. "You know my politics have not changed. I simply wish to see my friend prosper, and remain one of the city's leading merchant-traders."

"So what do you propose that I do?" Calvin asked, still smiling. "To solve the crisis caused by Mrs. Soule's departure and to keep me among New York's first rank?"

"As it so happens, I know of a fine candidate for her replacement. Mrs. Katharine Daly. A widow. A very respectable woman. She's a hard worker, she cooks well, and she's very intelligent."

"I see," Calvin said, suddenly suspicious. He did his best to steer clear of his friend's tangled romantic life. Livingston was notorious for his fleeting attachments to serving girls, tavern wenches, and other available females. "How old is this widow? And what is your connection with her?"

"It's not like that," Rhodes said, reddening. "Not at all, if that's what you're suggesting. I met her through Mr. O'Connor. She's from Dublin. As to her age, I would guess that she's nearing thirty years."

"Friends with Francis O'Connor? Isn't he a firebrand for Theobald Wolfe Tone and the United Irishmen?"

Rhodes nodded, adjusting his spectacles. "I believe that O'Connor is related to Mrs. Daly. A distant relation."

"Would this Mrs. Daly share O'Connor's revolutionary beliefs, by any chance?"

"She's Irish, Calvin. I can't imagine that she would feel warmly toward the British, not with the current state of affairs. But that's neither here nor there."

"As you know, I live a quiet life by choice. I have little or no appetite for introducing misguided revolutionary fervor into my kitchen or my parlor."

"I'm not proposing that a female Tom Paine join your household. She'll cook and clean and wash. Mrs. Daly is struggling to make ends meet, and she would welcome honest employment and a roof over her head. I thought you would be sympathetic. Will you at least interview her for the position? As a favor to me?"

"Of course I shall interview her, and I'm sympathetic. But let her know, gently, that a condition of the job is that she must stay clear of politics. Tarkington & Scott does a lucrative business with British merchants. I can't have it said that my housekeeper is openly agitating against the Crown or that I'm harboring Irish radicals in my home. She must understand that."

"That goes without saying." Rhodes smiled. "I think you'll like her, Calvin. She's a high-spirited woman."

"I'm sure she is. Anything else about her I should know?"

"She comes from a Protestant family, not that she's a church-goer."

Calvin snorted. "I'm hiring a housekeeper, not a deacon. There's no religious test, Livingston. You know I don't share your concerns about Rome."

"It's not Catholics *per se*," Livingston said. "It's the Pope and the priests, the ones who promote superstition and submission."

"Rest easy, then. Mrs. Daly poses no threat of turning me into a Papist. Bring her by the house."

Livingston grinned. "Care to join me at Martling's for a tankard or two of ale?"

Calvin picked up his copy of the *Odyssey* from the desk. "To tell the truth, Livingston, I'd prefer to get back to Ithaca. Odysseus the *polytropos*—the man driven off course—is about to stand with Telemachus and confront the suitors in the Great Hall. It's Homer at his best."

* * *

A day later Livingston Rhodes again knocked at Calvin's study door, this time accompanied by a tall, auburn-haired woman. Katharine Daly proved to be quite handsome, with green, alert eyes, a full mouth, and a ready smile. She wore her hair in a chignon that exposed her neck. Calvin was surprised—based on Livingston's brief description, he had expected an older female worn down by her cares, not a poised and attractive young woman.

"This is quite a library, Mr. Tarkington," she said after the introductions, glancing around at his crowded bookshelves. "As fine as any I've seen in Dublin."

Calvin had shipped the library from Boston to Greenwich Street. It had been Phillip Tarkington's pride and joy, and Calvin's father had filled it with an eclectic mixture of theological tomes and maritime books. Calvin's contribution to the crowded shelves had been leather-bound volumes of many of the classical authors from Rome and Greece, a large collection of books about China in French and English, and the works of

Edmund Burke, Adam Smith, John Locke, Jonathan Swift, John Dunne, and, of course, William Shakespeare.

"I've a pronounced weakness for books," Calvin replied. "I find them hard to resist."

"The clerks at Gaine's and McKean's know him well," Rhodes said. "I'd wager that Calvin keeps half the booksellers in New York solvent."

"It's a fine weakness, as weaknesses go," she said.

Calvin smiled. "I'm glad I have your approval."

He waved them into the chairs facing his writing desk. "How long have you been in America, Mrs. Daly?"

"Four years now," she said. "We lived in Philadelphia until my husband returned to Ireland last year. Then word came that he had died. It was a considerable shock. My kinsman Francis O'Connor suggested that I move here to New York."

"I'm sorry for your loss. What was your husband's profession?"

"He was a solicitor. But first and foremost, a patriot, an Irish patriot." She glanced over at Livingston, weighing her words. "I'll not hide the fact that I believe he was murdered by the authorities in Ireland. Dublin Castle has moved against anyone suspected of supporting independence. It's bad enough in the city, but the Orangemen run riot in the countryside against those accused of assisting the United Irishmen. Beatings, imprisonment, killings. All of this outside of the law."

"You have my condolences," Calvin said to her. "You're young to suffer such a loss."

She took a moment to adjust her chignon. "You understand, though, how these things can happen," she said. "According to Mr. Rhodes, you were in Paris together during the French Revolution."

"We saw some of the excesses there," Calvin said. "In fact, I've witnessed two revolutions. Ours here in America, and the French one. One triumphant and one tragic."

"Noble intentions in both cases," Rhodes said. "Noble causes." He turned to Calvin. "There's grim news from Ireland in the London papers that just arrived. A rising in County Kildare suppressed. Lord Fitzgerald betrayed to the British, dead by his own hand. The rebels in County Wexford are fighting, though. It's a shame that Wolfe Tone is in France. I believe that Irishmen would rally to his banner."

"He is a great man." Katharine Daly's eyes shone with emotion. "Mr. Tone is our best hope for Ireland."

"I've read some of his essays," Calvin said. "He makes cogent arguments for ending religious persecution, for reforming Parliament, and for Ireland's independence. I have no quarrel with any of that. Nonetheless, if you're to work for me, you cannot be seen as agitating publicly for the Irish cause. My firm has dealings with British merchants and with the East India Company."

"I explained that to Mrs. Daly," Rhodes said.

"I'd like to hear her thoughts on the question, if you don't mind, Livingston."

"You would have me stay silent on the injustices in Ireland?" she asked, coloring. "Do you know what has been transpiring there? The persecution? The killings?"

"We're an ocean away from Dublin," Calvin said. "We sit here in Manhattan in the state of New York. Our republic is not at war with Great Britain."

"Are you indifferent to this injustice, then?"

"Katharine, really," Rhodes said.

Calvin silenced him with a look. "I want Mrs. Daly to speak her mind, Livingston. I'm not indifferent to the situation in Ireland, but I've traveled far and wide enough to learn that the world is filled with injustice. I believe we must start at home, and do what we can to improve matters where we live."

"Where do you stand on slavery in your own country, then, if I may inquire?" she asked, the color still in her face.

"Slavery? My family has never held slaves. Never will. I've supported the

Manumission Society. It was founded to try to end slavery, and while Governor Jay has proposed two bills to do that, they haven't passed the General Assembly. Yet I'm confident that gradual abolition will be accomplished in the future, and peacefully."

"There was no yellow fever in New York before they brought the slaves here from the West Indies," she said. "Some claim the deaths from the fever are God's way of showing disapproval."

Calvin shook his head. "Dr. Bayley says the slaves didn't bring the fever. It's been caused by the noxious vapors from the marshy land by the East River. No divine retribution involved."

"I long ago gave up hope of a righteous God settling scores," Livingston said. "At least in this world, if not the next."

"If the slaves in this city had the means to end their bondage, I'm sure they would," Katharine said. "They wouldn't wait on divine intervention. We Irish certainly can't, and we won't."

Calvin frowned. "Discretion is often the better part of valor. Livingston speaks highly of you, Mrs. Daly, and that carries great weight with me. I don't think that it's unreasonable to ask that you refrain from political agitation while in my household. Those must be my conditions for your employment."

She took a deep breath. "I will accept them, Mr. Tarkington. While I am under your roof, or in your offices, I will not openly agitate for my country's independence."

"That's a solicitor's phrasing," Calvin said with a thin smile. "I would seek your promise that, regardless of your location, you will not entangle this household or Tarkington & Scott in Irish politics."

She tossed her head. "I understand. No public agitation. There will be no repercussions for you or your firm. I can promise that as well."

"It's settled then," Livingston said quickly. "Mrs. Daly will prove to be a fine housekeeper, Calvin. I know that you'll be pleased."

"I'm sure that I shall," Calvin said, turning to her. "When would it be convenient for you to start?"

"There's no point in waiting," she said briskly. "If you'll show me the way to the kitchen, I'll see about supper."

Calvin was amused. "Tomorrow would be fine," he said. "We can send a man for your things. There are servants' quarters near the kitchen. A small bedroom, but it has a fireplace that keeps it tolerably warm in the winter."

"Thank you," she said. "Expect me in the morning, then."

"Not even a passing interest in what you'll be paid?" Calvin asked, arching his eyebrows.

She gave him a broad smile, her mood changed. "Livingston said that you would be more than fair. In fact, he suggested that you were known for overpaying your servants, and your firm's employees."

"An exaggeration," Rhodes said, flushing. "I don't think I said exactly that."

"I have no doubt that you did," Calvin said. "But I'd rather have a reputation for generosity than not. And there is a method in my madness—my 'overpaid' employees are loyal to a fault."

After Livingston and Mrs. Daly had left, Calvin sat at his desk in his study, wondering whether he had made a mistake. Would she chafe at her role as his housekeeper? Katharine Daly wasn't the only well-bred newcomer to New York to have fallen in station. Since the French Revolution and the slave uprising in Saint-Domingue, the city had been filled with displaced aristocrats and once-wealthy merchants and their families.

Hereditary titles and polished manners didn't put bread on the table, and it wasn't uncommon to find a count giving dancing lessons or a once wealthy matron making ends meet by her sewing. Some less fortunate women resorted to prostitution, working in the brothels near St. Paul's Church that catered to the wealthy, or if they had lost their looks, walking the streets near the Battery and the docks.

Calvin was intrigued by Katharine Daly. It was clear that she needed the job, but she had resisted before accepting his conditions. He liked her spirit, her independence. He did question, however, whether those were the best qualities for the servant meant to keep his house.

* * *

It was a gray afternoon, but there was time for Calvin to visit Sarah's grave before dark. It had been a month since he had gone to the Beth a Haim, at Pearl and Chatham Streets, the small graveyard for New York's Jews, to pay his respects.

When he reached the cemetery, a simple field lined with gravestones next to the Rutgers family's farmhouse, he found the gate in the whitewashed fence was unlatched. He glanced up briefly at the sky, noting that the clouds had grown darker. Rain was coming.

He walked over to Sarah's gravestone, and the painful memories of her funeral came flooding back—the halting of the procession seven times, the mourners tearing their clothing, the ten solemn-faced men reciting the Kaddish at the grave site, the immediate covering of Sarah's coffin with dirt.

After the ceremony, Calvin had only indistinct memories. He remembered his friend Richard Varick guiding him to a waiting carriage and then the agony of the first night, when he could not sleep, even though he was exhausted.

Calvin had stayed with Sarah's father as he sat shiva, and then retreated into his own days of despair. He had turned to the bottle. The days had passed in a blur. Only the preparations for the voyage to China had lifted him out of darkness.

Much later, he had stumbled across a saying from a Spanish rabbi, "It is a fearful thing to love what death can touch." That thought had stayed with him in the years since losing Sarah.

He stood before her gravestone, and thought about her grace and beauty. They had been about to embark on a life together—she had fallen ill only months before their planned wedding—and the sudden fever that killed her, had also killed that future.

Calvin didn't believe in a Supreme Being who cared about his creations. He had lost his faith at the age of twelve when cancer had consumed his mother. He had seen little since to convince him that he was in error—in one sense, Sarah's senseless death hadn't surprised him. If he believed in anything, it was in the randomness of life—and, as the Stoics instructed, in the virtue of accepting whatever hand he might be dealt by Fate.

He heard the rumbling of distant thunder. Calvin reached into his coat pocket and retrieved a small stone he had brought from the backyard garden at Greenwich Street. He carefully placed it on the top of Sarah's gravestone. Then, it was time to leave.

THREE

Calvin found the sudden introduction of Katharine Daly into his daily life a disturbing, but not unwelcome, change. He had become so used to the matronly presence of Mrs. Soule that he was unsettled by how it felt having an attractive woman around at such close quarters.

When he and Katharine were alone in the house, there was an intimacy of sorts that he had not fully anticipated. He had not thought of himself as lonely—he had his books, and his work, and his circle of friends—but Katharine's presence made him realize what he had been missing. He was immediately attracted to her, and he believed she felt something as well—more than once he had caught her looking at him before she quickly averted her eyes.

He found himself wondering what it would be like to kiss her lips, to embrace her, to make love to her. He tried not to think of it—he didn't need the complications of an affair, let alone one with a servant, no matter how alluring she might be.

Despite his better judgment, he wanted to know more about her. He was by nature curious, and she intrigued him. On her third night of employment, he invited her to eat dinner with him.

She surveyed him coolly and replied to his invitation with a question. "Did Mrs. Soule sit with you at table?"

"She did not," he admitted. "She also did not read the newspapers, nor have any interest in the events of the day, so our conversation would have been quite limited. Livingston tells me that you take a keen interest in these matters."

"I do, indeed," she said, and hesitated. "It would perhaps be best if I have a cup of coffee with you, when you have finished your meal. I wouldn't want people to think there was a greater familiarity, and draw the wrong conclusions."

"As you wish," he said. "I'm sure you've heard Livingston quote Shakespeare that things are only as we make them."

"There's some truth to that," she said. "But I know how people are, and a woman's reputation can be falsely damaged by idle talk."

Calvin nodded. "Then we'll have coffee together, and talk about the events of the day."

She smiled and tucked a loose strand of hair behind her ear. "I would like that."

* * *

In the days that followed, Calvin found himself looking forward to their after-dinner chats. He discovered that Katharine knew a great deal about the world, and—as he had first learned during their interview—she had a mind of her own. She naturally took the side of the common man or woman, and she wasn't afraid to challenge Calvin when she thought he was wrong.

He admired her passion, and was relieved that it was tempered by her sense of humor. She had a quick wit, and had deftly skewered him more than once. As he got to know her, he found that she had a playful side, as well.

It was several weeks before she asked him about Sarah, although she did so carefully and indirectly.

Over coffee, he had related the story of how he had moved Tarkington & Scott's offices from near Boston's Long Wharf to Manhattan. A lucrative voyage to China had allowed Calvin to purchase another ship, a brig, and to begin trading with the West Indies. In turn, the firm had greatly prospered over the past several years.

"Livingston claims that you're the canniest trader in New York," she said.

"I doubt that."

"He says that a drawback of your recent prosperity is that now the matrons of New York society have designs on you for their daughters."

"Designs on me?" Calvin shook his head. "Livingston shouldn't repeat idle gossip. He has told you something of my history, no doubt. Perhaps too much. Consequently, you probably know that I lost my intended, Miss Hays, to a sudden fever four years ago. Then I left New York for the voyage to China. Since my return, I've been preoccupied with business matters. As I have remained unattached, I'm an obvious target for those matrons Livingston talks about. They'll be disappointed, however, as I'm quite happy in my current state."

"You've no intention of marrying, then?"

"I do not. Surely Livingston told you that as well."

"He did." She paused, hesitant. "He said that it's because you compare every woman you meet to Miss Hays, and that they inevitably fall short."

Calvin frowned. "Livingston forgets himself."

"My apologies. He thinks the world of you. Please don't be cross with him about this. I pressed him on the subject."

"Did you?" Calvin arched his eyebrows.

She colored. "Considering my current station in life, you can imagine why I might want to learn more about the character of my prospective employer. There are men in this city—married men—who would seek to take advantage of my circumstances if I came under their roof. Livingston assured me that would never happen with you."

Calvin glanced at her, softening. "Yes, it's natural that you would want to make inquiries. Did his explanation for my bachelorhood satisfy your curiosity?"

"To some degree. I think that I better understand your situation. As a widow, I'm familiar with some of the emotions. We differ, perhaps, in that I hope to remarry some day, to have children. And my husband was no paragon of virtue, so comparisons wouldn't be as troublesome."

"Livingston is wrong about the question of comparisons. In China, I met a remarkable young woman. In some ways, she was as different from Sarah as night and day, but in others they were sisters."

"Livingston said nothing of her."

"For good reason. He knows nothing about her."

"What is her name?" she asked softly.

"Eldedei." Calvin realized he had never spoken her name to anyone in New York before. He wondered why he had chosen to confide in Katharine, a woman he had known only a few weeks.

"Do you exchange letters with her? Is that possible?"

"No letters," he said. "Perhaps someday I'll tell you the story, with your promise that you won't share it with Livingston."

"Mr. Tarkington," she said. "You may trust me to keep your confidences, small and large."

"I am learning that, Mrs. Daly," he said. "I believe that I can trust you."

* * *

Calvin was slightly embarrassed when, a week later, there came proof positive of his perceived matrimonial eligibility. Richard and Maria Varick came calling on a surprisingly brisk Wednesday afternoon with Miss Grace Roosevelt in tow, a distant cousin of Maria's who was visiting from Albany.

Maria Varick's cousin was very pretty, a petite woman with long dark hair that fell to her shoulders in ringlets. Calvin guessed that she was nineteen or twenty years old.

He showed them into the parlor, and then excused himself long enough to find Katharine and ask her to bring them tea. When he returned, his guests were discussing what books Grace might read for her improvement.

"Perhaps *Pilgrim's Progress* would fit the bill," Varick said. "What do you think, Calvin?"

Calvin turned to her. "What are your interests, Miss Roosevelt?" he asked.

"I would like to know more about other lands," Grace said. "This is the first time I've been more than fifty miles from Albany. I understand from my uncle that you have sailed to the four corners of the earth."

He smiled. "Not quite that far. Perhaps to the two corners of the earth. Europe, China, and the West Indies."

"You have been to London and Paris? By all accounts they are filled with grand buildings and multitudes of people from all walks of life."

"Of the two, I prefer Paris, although I prefer New York as a much better place to live."

"Even New York seems the grand city to me," she said. "Of course, that is in comparison to Albany."

"If you want to read about the world, I'd recommend *Gulliver's Travels*. It's fantastical, of course, but Mr. Swift captures quite well the strangeness of travel, encountering new people and customs. Then there's Captain Cook and Boswell and Miss Wollstonecraft. I would be happy to lend you their books from my library. It will give me room for a few new volumes."

"I would like that very much," she said.

She was about to say more when they were interrupted by Katharine, who arrived carrying a silver tray with a teapot and cups.

"My new housekeeper," Calvin said in way of an introduction. "Mrs. Daly. She came to my rescue when Mrs. Soule abandoned us for her family in Philadelphia."

Maria Varick acknowledged her with a slight nod, and Calvin noticed that she watched Katharine intently as she gracefully poured their tea.

"I can't imagine why Mrs. Soule would ever abandon such a pleasant home," Maria said, exchanging a quick glance with her husband.

"Her daughter in Philadelphia had twins," Calvin said. "A sound reason to weigh anchor."

Katharine finished serving their tea, curtsied, and left the parlor. Richard Varick watched her until she had disappeared behind the door leading to the kitchen.

"Quite different from Mrs. Soule," he said.

"She is, indeed," Calvin said. "She's Irish. Livingston Rhodes introduced her to me. She lost her husband, and needed a position."

"You were in luck, then," Varick said. "Good servants are hard to find. Yet I suspect that you aren't particularly demanding of your help."

"It's true that I rarely entertain, and keeping house for me is relatively simple."

"Richard complains that we haven't had you to our home for dinner in some time," Maria said. "Would you be available next week? Wednesday or Thursday? Grace will join us."

"Thank you for the invitation," Calvin replied. "Why don't we plan on Wednesday? And I'll bring the books for Grace, then."

"Thank you, Mr. Tarkington," she said, smiling. "It gives us all something to look forward to."

* * *

The following weeks found Calvin fielding numerous invitations from the Varicks. He declined most, but not wanting to offend Richard—a longtime friend of the Tarkington family—he agreed to another dinner and an outing to the country with Grace and the Varicks.

She was a sweet, well-bred young woman, but Calvin quickly discovered that she couldn't carry her end of a conversation about anything more consequential than upcoming balls or the latest fashions. She had struggled when he asked her about *Gulliver's Travels*—Swift's satire was lost on her, and she didn't make the connection between his whimsical societies and the world around her. Calvin had told Katharine that he tried to avoid comparisons, but he couldn't help but contrast Grace's shallow interests with those of his housekeeper.

Richard Varick had known Calvin long enough to realize that he would never choose Grace Roosevelt for his wife, no matter how young and lovely she was—the matchmaking had all been of Maria's doing. Calvin was careful not to raise Grace's hopes. He remained pleasant but distant, and made sure he was never alone with her. He was quite relieved when Maria announced that her cousin would be returning to Albany.

He was surprised by the next, unexpected turn of events. Katharine knocked on his study door on the Thursday morning after Grace had left New York and asked if they could talk.

"Of course, what is it?" He put down the ledger book he was reviewing and motioned her to sit. She shook her head and remained standing.

"I must give my notice, Mr. Tarkington."

"Your notice? What's wrong?"

She pursed her lips. "Nothing of concern to you. I have my reasons. Private reasons."

"I wish to respect your privacy, but this is quite sudden and unwelcome. Can you be persuaded to reconsider?"

She shook her head for a second time.

"There may be talk," Calvin said. "Not that I give a damn, but you can understand that your sudden departure from my employ will raise questions. If you were a mature woman, like Mrs. Soule, it would be one thing. But you're young and handsome, and there's bound to be gossip."

"Does that bother you?" she asked. "The thought of gossip about us?"

"I don't worry about gossip. I live as I please. But you know that the world judges a woman differently, and a reputation, once damaged, is difficult to repair. I would never want that for you. I cannot compel you to stay, but I'm sorely disappointed, to say the least. I'm prepared to pay you more, if that's the issue."

"You have been more than generous. My wages are not the issue. I have come to realize that I'm ill-suited for this work."

"Yet you've been quite good at it." He found himself staring at her, not sure what to think, conscious that he was both annoyed and disturbed by the turn of events. "Would you at least stay until I can arrange for another housekeeper?"

She gave him a quick nod, and he noticed tears welling in her eyes.

Calvin was frustrated by her unwillingness to explain her reasons for leaving. He departed the house in a foul mood, and walked over to Martling's Tavern on Nassau Street where he found Livingston Rhodes with a full tankard of ale and copies of the latest news sheets spread before him on the table. Calvin joined him and quickly explained the situation.

"Can you stop by the house and talk to her, Livingston?" he asked. "Find out why she wants to leave. I'll be damned if I understand it. She's doing a capable job, and I have no complaints."

"I can try," he said. "I'm perplexed, to be honest. I can't imagine what she might be thinking to leave like this."

Calvin watched as his friend left the inn, somewhat unsteady on his feet. He then ordered ale, and nursed his drink for an hour while he waited for Livingston's return, thinking about Katharine and his growing attraction to her. He had been careful not to cross any lines with her. While Calvin had resisted imagining a future with her, now he found he couldn't envision one without her.

The tavern door swung open, and Livingston reappeared. He caught Calvin's eye and shook his head in apparent regret as he made his way to the table. He had the barmaid fill his tankard and took a long swig of ale before he spoke.

"She won't say directly what's at issue," he said. "She's vague. Evasive. Not uncommon when a woman feels wronged."

"Wronged? Is it because I have kept her from politics? From agitating for the Irish cause?"

"I think not." Rhodes paused to drink some of his ale. "She seems concerned about a possible change in your household arrangements. The prospects of a new mistress at Greenwich Street."

"What? Absurd."

Livingston rubbed his nose. "There has been some talk about you and Miss Roosevelt. Dinner at the Varicks. A picnic. A carriage ride or two around town. I've heard the rumors myself."

"She's a pleasant enough young lady," Calvin said. Could Katharine be acting out of jealousy? It seemed so clear to him that if forced to choose, he would pick Katharine over Grace Roosevelt or any other woman in New York. "There's been no courtship. I have given Miss Roosevelt no cause to think otherwise. In fact, she's returned to Albany."

"That might make a difference with Katharine. It might indeed. I would recommend that you inform her. Forthwith."

"Livingston, I believe that you're in your cups."

"I may very well be, but that doesn't mean I'm wrong on this. In short, you've conquered her heart, Calvin, whether you intended to or not."

* * *

Calvin did as Livingston suggested when he returned to Greenwich Street and found Katharine in the kitchen, preparing dinner.

He asked her if they could talk further about her situation. "I've given some thought to your leaving, and I don't like it. Not a whit. I want you to stay." He looked at her directly. "I want you to know that I have no plans to alter my domestic arrangements. Livingston suggested that you had concerns on that account."

"I do," she said. "I doubt Miss Roosevelt would want me here, nor would that suit me. I wished to leave before that happened."

"It will not happen. I have no attachment to her. We've agreed that these comparisons are invidious, so I will only say that *your* qualities, Mrs. Daly, are more to my liking."

"What are you saying?" she asked.

"I'm saying that if I were of a mind to court a woman, it would be you."

She gasped, quickly covering her mouth with her hand, a look of dismay on her face. "And now you have made it quite impossible for me to stay here."

He smiled at her. "Impossible? Many things in life are impossible, but this does not seem to be one of them."

"Do you propose courting your housekeeper?" she asked, her face coloring. "My employer and my would-be lover? Consider my position."

"I have, Katharine," he said. He took her right hand in his. "I'm well past thirty. I know what I want, and so I will be direct. I believe that we're well matched in our interests, and I find you very appealing. In fact, I've wanted to kiss your lips for weeks and to take you to bed."

She looked at him intently. "It's no different for me. But I won't be your kept woman, nor will I let you break my heart."

"I wish neither. I'll make you Mrs. Tarkington, if you'll let me."

"Are you sure? I bring only myself."

"What more could I want?"

"The world will think that I've thrown myself at you for money and position."

"The world will be wrong."

She rose, on tiptoes, and kissed him full on the mouth. "Come to bed, then, Calvin," she said.

She took her apron off and kissed him again. They hurried up the stairwell together, eager to reach the bedroom.

* * *

They spent most of the weekend in Calvin's four-poster bed, delighting in the novelty of each other's nakedness. He marveled at Katharine's unpinned auburn hair as it covered his pillow, and the softness of her lightly freckled skin. He made her laugh when he buried his face in her hair and then kissed her neck, chin, nose, and forehead. She matched his eagerness in bed, and he realized how starved for the touch of a lover he had been.

They talked quietly, hand-in-hand, bodies touching, between frantic bouts of making love. She told him about her Dublin childhood as the only daughter of John Connaughton, a Trinity College professor of Rhetoric and Philosophy. Her father had introduced Katharine to the world of ideas early on, encouraging her to lose herself in his vast collection of books and insisting that she think for herself. She had been nineteen when she met Sean Daly, a charming and energetic man eight years her senior, a man unlike any she had encountered during her sheltered upbringing.

She had accepted his marriage proposal, and it was six months into the marriage that she realized that Sean's charm was coupled with impulsive recklessness. He had left a string of angry creditors—tailors, hatmakers, innkeepers, landlords—across Dublin. It had been hard for her—she was often ashamed when they had to hurriedly leave their lodgings, one step ahead of a bill collector.

When Sean had joined the underground movement for Irish independence, she had hoped that it would curb his restlessness. She had shared his distaste for the oppression of Irish Catholics and the obvious injustice of British rule, but she began to wonder whether he was drawn more by the excitement of taking risks than the loftier goal of a free Ireland. She had resolved to see it through with him, and had willingly accompanied him when he followed Theobald Wolfe Tone to the United States.

"When he returned to Ireland at Mr. Tone's direction last year, Sean convinced me to remain in Philadelphia," she explained. "He felt it would be too dangerous for me. We quarreled. Even when I learned that he had been betrayed to the authorities, I was convinced that he would somehow talk his way out of the trap. Of course, that wasn't the case. Word came that he had been hung by the British."

"At first, I didn't believe it," she continued. "He seemed indestructible. Then it was reported in the Dublin newspapers that he had died in custody." She sighed. "He was a flawed man, and not a responsible husband, but there were happy times in the marriage. Then I came to New York, hoping to start over."

"When I met you, I fought against the attraction. Other men had courted me, but it was too soon after Sean, and I promised myself I wouldn't rush into marriage out of loneliness. A married man or two propositioned me, as you might expect, but I set them right immediately."

"I've been unlucky in love," he replied. "Until now. Who would have thought that Mrs. Soule's decision to leave my employ would have such marvelous consequences? I should not be surprised. There has been no straight path in my life."

She listened intently as he told her about the two women in his past—Sarah Gomez Hays, the daughter of a Philadelphia merchant, and Eldedei, the widow of a Manchu warrior.

"They were as different as night and day," he said. "Yet they shared the courage to love fully and without fear."

"And you lost them both," she said, running her hand slowly across his naked chest.

"That I did."

"You will not lose me," she said fiercely. "Not if it is within my power."

"Nor mine," he said.

"I worry for you," she said. "The scars on your body."

"You've read the *Odyssey*? My scars are not from a boar's tusk, like Odysseus. They're from old battles, and perhaps one day I can tell you their provenance. But not now. I have other matters I would prefer to discuss with you." He slowly moved his hand down her stomach.

"To discuss?"

"In a manner of speaking," he said.

* * *

They were married in the front parlor of the Greenwich Street house in a simple civil ceremony, with Richard Varick officiating in his capacity as mayor of New York. Calvin dressed in his best suit, and Katharine wore a simple white muslin dress embroidered in satin stitch.

Maria Varick, Jean Laurent, and Livingston Rhodes witnessed the brief ceremony, and then they all climbed into carriages to make the short trip to Fraunces Tavern, where they enjoyed a celebratory dinner in a private room.

Livingston was on his best behavior; he refrained from debating politics with the staunchly Federalist Varick, and he honored the couple with an Irish toast: "May the saddest day of your future be no worse than the happiest day of your past."

Later, when Calvin and Katharine had returned to Greenwich Street, they sat together for a moment in the parlor. Katharine mentioned how relieved she had been by her kind treatment by Maria Varick.

She sighed. "I realized that I had the deepest feeling for you when Mrs. Varick brought that Roosevelt girl for tea in this very room. I remember glancing at her and thinking that she was so young and pretty and that you would fall for her, and I felt true despair. What chance did I have?"

"I was being polite," Calvin said. "They have been loyal friends, and I couldn't very well slight them when they came calling."

"You saw her more than once, did you not? Didn't you enjoy having her hanging on every word? Did you imagine her as your wife?"

'I had no intention of marrying. I didn't plan to wed Miss Roosevelt or anyone else, despite what others may have thought." He paused. "I hope you're not jealous. Not now."

"She was so proper and conventional, and I was certain that you would be bored with her in six months. That would serve you right for choosing her, for stupidly preferring a slip of a child to a woman with a mind of her own."

"Such righteous anger," Calvin said with a smile. "May I remind you that I chose you? Clearly, there's something to be said for pretty red-haired widows, even those with quick tempers."

"Don't you dare smirk at me, Calvin Tarkington," she said. "Imagine if I hadn't threatened to leave? We wouldn't be standing here, married, and you'd be missing out on your wedding night."

"And that would have been a true tragedy, Mrs. Tarkington," he said, taking her into his arms.

FOUR

At first, Calvin thought that he was hearing the sound of thunder, for it had been raining most of the day; a storm had swept in from the harbor unexpectedly and drenched New York in a curtain of cold rain. When he had looked out through the rain-streaked front parlor window earlier in the afternoon, he could see that wide puddles covered a large stretch of Greenwich Street in front of his house.

The pounding noise continued, and then Calvin recognized that the sound was not thunder, but someone knocking on the front door of the house. He had been perched on the large overstuffed Hepplewhite wingback chair in the parlor, a volume of *The Enchiridion* open before him.

He quickly checked his pocket watch, a French verge with the seal of the Society of Cincinnati engraved on its gold cover, a gift from his older brother, and found that it was almost half past seven o'clock. Calvin had been so caught up in his own thoughts that he had not heard the bracket clock on the mantel striking the hour. He cursed and struggled to his feet and found his way to the foyer.

"I'm coming," he called out irritably. "Cease that damn pounding."

Whoever was on the other side of the door must have heard him, for the noise stopped. Calvin fumbled with the front-door latch, cursing again, and managed to pull the door open; his reward was a spray of cold rain from outside. A tall young man stood there before him, still partially exposed to the rain, which continued to pour down. The man wore the garb of a frontiersman: a coarse linen hunting shirt belted at the waist, breeches, leather leggings, and moccasins. A tomahawk and hunting bag, with an attached powder horn, hung from his leather belt and a broad-brimmed hat kept the rain off his face. The stranger gripped a long flintlock rifle in his right hand, with its muzzle pointed down.

"Calvin Tarkington?" the man asked. "Is this Mr. Tarkington's house?"

Calvin stared at the stranger. "It is, and I'm Calvin Tarkington. And who might you be, if I might inquire?"

"Barnabas Hardwick," the man said. He touched the brim of his hat, displacing some of the rain collected there. Water dripped onto the steps in front of them. "A friend of Judah Gomez."

"Judah Gomez?" Calvin asked, confused. He had last seen Judah, Sarah's cousin, six years ago in France. "Do you bring word from Paris?"

"Paris? No, I've come from the Ohio country, the Northwest Territory, where Judah lives."

"Come in, then," Calvin said. He opened the door wider and let the man step inside into the foyer.

In the light of the hallway lamp, Calvin saw that the man was younger than he had first appeared, perhaps in his mid-twenties.

Katharine must have heard their voices because she appeared in the hallway. She looked at Hardwick's muddy leggings and moccasins with dismay.

Calvin made the introductions, and Hardwick gave her a short bow.

"Have you had supper?" she asked.

When Hardwick shook his head, she insisted that they move to the kitchen, where she set a plate for him at the table-board. He smiled broadly for the first time when she brought him a pewter tankard of cider. Calvin sat down across from him. Katharine filled Hardwick's plate with a large helping of beef stew and a chunk of bread she had warmed in the Dutch oven.

Calvin waited until Hardwick had finished his meal before he asked about Judah Gomez. Hardwick located his saddlebags at his feet and hunted through them for a moment, apparently finding what he had been seeking. He straightened up and handed Calvin a grubby envelope.

Calvin opened it and found a letter of two pages, written in French. He read the letter quickly.

Dear Calvin,

I trust that this missive finds you well. I write to you from the Northwest Territory.

You may remember that more than once on our trip from Paris to Perpignan, you suggested that I might find a new homeland in America. I decided to leave France in the spring of '95, when the Revolution, like Atlas, began devouring its own children.

When I arrived in Philadelphia, I learned from Abraham Hays of my dear cousin Sarah's death a year earlier. You can imagine my shock and sorrow, although I know it must have been a fraction of what you must have felt. Abraham, in poor health, died shortly before I left for the frontier.

Yes, I decided to seek my fortune in the West. I journeyed to Gallipolis, the colony of my countrymen and women on the Ohio River, and lived there for a time.

Then, on a trip to the town of Cincinnati, I met Rachel and fell in love. We married, and have a daughter, Naomi, and live in Canaan, a settlement near Fort Hamilton established by Rachel's father, Daniel Flint.

Now, my friend Calvin, I must ask for your help. I have fallen ill, and I wish to return East, to Philadelphia, and seek the care of the physician Benjamin Rush, who is said to work wonders with ailments such as mine.

My request is simple. Would you come to Canaan and accompany us—for I wish to bring Rachel and Naomi with me—on the trip to Philadelphia? If, for whatever reason, I cannot complete this journey, your presence would ensure the safety and well-being of my family.

Barnabas knows the way, and you can trust him.

With the hope of seeing you in person.

Your friend,

Judah

Calvin sat for a moment, collecting his thoughts. He had been surprised by the strange messenger, and he had been unprepared for the message he carried. He turned to Hardwick.

"Judah is sick."

Hardwick nodded. "His stomach. He's been losing weight, and he's faring poorly."

Calvin turned to a puzzled Katharine and explained that Sarah's cousin had written from the Northwest Territory, and had asked for Calvin's assistance in bringing his family to Philadelphia.

He turned back to Hardwick. "How do you know Judah?"

"I was hunting on contract for the Army at Fort Washington, out of Cincinnati, when I met Judah. That's how I first heard of Canaan."

"Do you live in Canaan?"

"I've a cabin near Judah's where I've been staying of late, but I wouldn't say that I live there."

"How large a town is it?" Katharine asked.

"It's not a town, ma'am. A few cabins about a few miles or so from the Miami River, near enough for the better soil but not so close that the cabins get flooded out. Daniel Flint, Rachel's father, named it Canaan, after the land of milk and honey."

"I'm curious," Katharine said. "Why did not Judah and his family come east with you on this trip?"

Hardwick shifted in his seat. "Judah didn't think we should leave Old Man Flint alone in Canaan. He must be close to seventy."

"Why couldn't he come to Philadelphia as well?" she asked.

"Daniel Flint is the most stubborn man I know. He's bound and determined to stay in Canaan. It's the Lord's will, the way he sees it. Rachel wouldn't leave her father unless she was sure that someone would be there to stay behind and watch over him. I've agreed to do that."

Katharine started to say something, and then stopped.

"Before I can travel, I must attend to some matters here in New York," Calvin said.

"I've not taken lodgings in New York," Hardwick said. "I came directly here. Judah hoped that you would return with me without delay."

"You must stay with us," Katharine said. "Until this is settled. There's a bedroom here, next to the kitchen."

"Thank you, Mrs. Tarkington," Hardwick said. "I could use a good night's sleep."

* * *

Once they were alone in the upstairs bedroom, Katharine did not hide her unhappiness with the situation.

"That young man may enjoy a good night's sleep," she said. "He has ruined mine. Must you take this trip?"

"I must," Calvin said. "I owe a great deal to Judah. He shielded me from the Jacobins, and saved my life in France. I wish that he had not asked for my help. Certainly not now, of all times, but I'm honor-bound to assist him."

"Why must you travel all the way there when Judah could have returned with this man Hardwick? It doesn't seem fair."

"Fair or not, Judah must have his reasons."

"I don't want you to go," she said. "And if you must, I want to come along, to accompany you."

"I would not subject you to the rigors of the journey."

"I wish to share those rigors."

He frowned. "The frontier is no place for a woman."

"Yet women live there, do they not?"

"A few," he conceded. "But not my wife. I would not want my beloved to be one of them. It can be a lawless place, and a dangerous one. Knowing that you are here, safe, waiting for me, will be best."

"I'm your wife," she said. "I'll do as you wish, although I'm not happy about this."

"I promise you that I'll return to New York as fast as possible," he said. "I need a day or two to resolve matters of business, and then I'll be off. The sooner I leave, the sooner I return."

* * *

In the morning, Calvin rose earlier than was his habit. He washed his face, carefully shaved, and put on clean body linen. He chose an expensive black waistcoat and tawny-colored breeches to go with his blue frock coat and clean, white stockings: he had business to attend to and he needed to be presentable.

His first destination was Tarkington & Scott's offices on Water Street, but he decided to stop by the docks on the East River first. In the past, he had found that he thought best when he walked along the waterfront. The smell of tar and fish and the river, the frenetic activity of the stevedores and shipmasters, the forest of masts rising into the sky, the stacked timber and masts in the small shipyard he passed, the sense of a port at work around him, all of it served to calm him with its familiarity.

Calvin took a deep breath of the sea air. He had always marveled at the ships from ports all over the world that found their way into New York's harbor from Europe and China, from the West and East Indies, from the literal ends of the earth. They carried goods and commodities of all kinds—textiles from England, porcelain from France, tea from China, molasses from the islands, spices from India—and somehow there was a ready market for them, willing buyers and sellers. Out from New York went timber, furs, gingko, silver, rum and other goods bound for anonymous merchants and traders in distant ports. The cycle of trade continued, come war or peace, hard times and good.

Over time Calvin had begun to take a quiet pride in the role that Tarkington & Scott played in that cycle of international commerce. New

York's shipping district was small compared to London's, but Calvin believed that someday his adopted city would compete for the trade of the world with London. As a port, New York had some natural advantages: a large harbor, and the potential for docks and wharfs on both the East and Hudson Rivers.

When he arrived at Tarkington & Scott's offices, he stopped first downstairs, where the company's clerks sat at several desks with their quills, inkstands, and sand boxes for blotting, close at hand. It was there that the often-voluminous paperwork of merchant trading was handled. He found Jean Laurent sitting near the front of the room, and took his friend aside. The Frenchman had been Tarkington & Scott's agent in France until the Jacobins assumed power, and he now watched over the finances and customs documents for the firm while also acting as ship's purser.

"I have word from Judah Gomez," Calvin said. The mention of Judah's name elicited a smile from Laurent.

"And how is M'sieu Judah?" Laurent asked. "It has been some time since I last heard his name."

"He has come to America, and needs my help. I must travel to the Ohio country."

"So you will be absent for some time?"

"That is so. While I'm gone, please ensure that Mrs. Tarkington has sufficient funds for her needs. I would also ask that you keep her informed of our affairs on a weekly basis. I'd like her to learn more about the workings of Tarkington & Scott. She's quite bright, and should pick it up quickly."

"As you wish, M'sieu Calvin."

He asked Laurent to send one of the office boys to Seth Elias' lodgings with the message that Calvin wished to see him. "And then have him stop by Martling's Tavern and fetch Livingston Rhodes," he said. "We have matters to discuss."

Calvin went to his own second floor office and occupied himself with paperwork while he waited for Elias. When Thomas Scott, his father's original partner, retired two years ago, Calvin had assumed responsibility for the firm and had managed it single-handedly since. His decision to aggressively pursue the China trade had paid off handsomely. In the past few years Tarkington & Scott had grown in size, and had become one of the more profitable firms in New York.

The firm had sent two ships to Canton since Calvin's initial risky trip in the *Liberty* in 1794. He employed Frederick Alsop, a well-regarded supercargo, to take the sloop back a year later, and had been pleased with the high quality of the tea, and the corresponding proceeds, when Alsop returned.

Elias had sailed Tarkington & Scott's new ship *Freedom* on its maiden voyage to China the following year. A 350-ton brigantine, *Freedom* had been specifically built for trading for tea; the ship's larger cargo space accommodated more than double the number of tea chests the *Liberty* could carry. As long as the New York market for tea remained strong, that larger tonnage would translate into commensurately larger profits for the firm.

When Seth Elias arrived, Calvin reviewed their plans for a spring voyage to Canton, when the winds in the Indian Ocean would be more favorable for those sailing by an eastern route. With any luck, Calvin would be back in New York long before Elias had to sail to China.

"What do you make of the news from Egypt?" Elias asked. "A great victory for the British and Lord Nelson, the newspapers say. The Battle of the Nile, the most successful engagement for the Royal Navy since the Glorious First of June. Could it be that this war nears its end?"

"I doubt that," Calvin said. "General Bonaparte has yet to lose any battles on land."

"French war ships continue to stop and board American merchantmen, a continuing insult to our sovereignty. They say President Adams is losing patience."

"He should take a page from President Washington's book. Washington kept us from entering the war in favor of France, and now Adams must keep us from joining Mr. Pitt and the British against the French."

After Elias had left, Calvin didn't have to wait too long before Livingston

Rhodes arrived. He quickly explained to his friend about the summons from Judah Gomez.

"What does Katharine say?" Livingston asked.

"She's not pleased, but she understands that I have a moral obligation to assist Judah. She worries about the dangers."

"Nothing will happen to you. You'll have your feet on solid ground the entire time. There's greater risk whenever you set sail, for then you're at the mercy of storm and tide."

"I know the sea. I'm ready for shoals or storms. It's different in the great forests."

"I'd offer to accompany you, but I'd make a poor companion in the wilderness. I'm no woodsman."

"You can do me a greater service here in New York. While I'm away, can you look in on Katharine? I've asked Jean to acquaint her with the basics of the firm's dealings—she has married a trader, after all. It will also keep her occupied so that she won't brood as much over my absence. But I will rely on you to help her if she encounters any unexpected difficulties."

"It would be my pleasure," Livingston said. "Of course, she must never know of your request, Calvin. Your wife wouldn't take kindly to the notion of someone looking after her. She's independent to a fault."

* * *

The following morning, when Calvin looked out onto Greenwich Street from his bedroom window, he could see that gray weather had returned. Dark clouds filled the sky, and the sun broke through only occasionally to glitter off the windows of the houses across the street. The air outside had turned noticeably colder.

When he arrived in the kitchen for breakfast, he learned that Barnabas Hardwick had already departed to run errands, leaving word that he would be back before ten o'clock.

Katharine proposed a carriage ride to the Battery and Calvin quickly agreed. They left the carriage near the northern end of the fortifications and walked to a vantage point with a view of the harbor. Calvin spotted the sails of a brig, headed east to sea, to the wide Atlantic.

"What do you think of young Mr. Hardwick?" Katharine asked him.

"He seems a capable sort."

"He says very little. When I tried to question him this morning about the Northwest, his answers were not very informative."

"A fish out of water," Calvin said. "He's not comfortable here, in the city. New York must be quite daunting."

"But he knows the frontier, enough to keep from being scalped."

Calvin fought back a smile. "The Ohio country has been free of Indian trouble for several years, now, since General Wayne signed the treaty at Greeneville. I should be able to keep my own hair."

"You joke, but I will worry. I don't like you being away from me for so long," she said. "It's a small thing, but I had hoped we could watch the leaves turn color. Enjoy the last of the fall."

"God willing, there will be other falls for us to enjoy. Doesn't absence make the heart grow fonder?"

"I can't imagine being any fonder of you than I already am."

"I'll take that as a challenge," Calvin replied. "You'll have to tell me upon my return. Better yet, show me."

* * *

In the evening, he prepared for the journey. Hardwick was eager to get an early start.

A glum Katharine served them a supper of fish chowder and freshly-baked bread. There was little conversation at the table and Calvin was thankful—he was in no mood for small talk.

When he packed his bag, he hesitated before the top dresser drawer, unsure whether he wanted to bring his pistol to the frontier. It was a small flintlock designed by the Bunney firm of London, meant to be carried in a man's pocket, hardly a weapon of much use in a wilderness. But he retrieved it from the drawer, smiling at his own superstitious belief that the pistol would somehow bring him luck.

Katharine went to bed early, but Calvin was restless and not ready for sleep. He left the bedroom and went downstairs to his study, where he lit two candles and found his copy of *The Enchiridion*. He sat at his desk and lost himself in the prose of Appian as he related the lessons he had been taught by Epictetus, the former slave who tutored a future emperor.

"Never say about anything, 'I have lost it'; but only, 'I have given it back.' Is your child dead? It has been given back. Is your wife dead? She has been given back."

Calvin stared at the Greek words on the page. Epictetus advised that man should not yearn for things beyond his own control, that the only peace in life could be found through inner serenity. Calvin looked for another passage he had marked.

"Do not seek to have everything that happens happen as you wish, but wish for everything to happen as it actually does happen and your life will be serene."

He found some comfort in that Stoic command. He would rely on Hardwick to guide him to the frontier, and—if all went as planned—he would accompany Judah and his family on the trip back to Philadelphia. He reminded himself there was no point in worrying about what he could not control—he would accept whatever Destiny had in store for him.

When he returned to the bedroom, Katharine stirred from sleep.

"There you are," she said with a slight smile. "Come back to bed, Calvin. Let me show you how fond of you I am. We must put to good use what little time we have until morning."

PART TWO

FIVE

It took sixteen days by coach, ferryboat, and horseback for Calvin and Barnabas Hardwick to reach the river town of Pittsburgh.

The vibrant autumn colors of the trees lining the turnpike from Philadelphia to Lancaster had transformed it into a corridor of bronze, crimson, and ocher. Calvin had taken it all in: the sharpened cries of migrating birds as they headed south, the smell of burning leaves, and the sight of wheels of baled hay in the nearby fields. As they neared Pittsburgh, the surrounding wooded hills presented a patchwork of scarlet maples, brown oaks, and evergreens—cedar, hemlock, and pine. He marveled at the dense forests with their towering trees, many reaching the height of the mainmast of a ship of the line.

He tried not to dwell too much on his separation from Katharine. He hated that he had to leave her alone so early in their married life, but he could never have turned his back on Judah when his friend was in need of help.

Calvin had been disappointed by his first glimpse of Pittsburgh, a once-famous British frontier outpost named after a prime minister who, had he lived, might have averted the bitter war between Britain and her colonies. The town was no more than a cluster of ramshackle log and frame buildings centered around four narrow muddy streets—Water, Market, Second, and Ferry. Near the river came the sound of hammering and sawing from several shipyards. To the north of the town stood Fort Fayette, with its log palisades and blockhouses, built a few years earlier, yet already looking shabby and ramshackle.

Calvin had expected something grander, a town on a larger scale, as would befit a place where two major rivers, the Monongahela and Allegheny, converged to form a third, the Ohio, a place which had been contested by the British and the French in their struggle for control of the West. When he voiced his disappointment, Hardwick laughed at him.

"Wait until we reach Cincinnati," he said. "This place is a metropolis in comparison."

After they had arranged for rooms at the Sign of the General Butler, on the east side of Market Street and left their luggage, Barnabas suggested that they visit the workshop of a skilled gunsmith, Mr. Kleber, where Calvin could purchase a long rifle.

"What's the saying—when in Rome do as the Romans do?" Barnabas grinned at him. "A rifle comes in handy."

They found Kleber, a stocky German with a thatch of salt-and-pepper colored hair, in one of the frame houses on Second Street; he welcomed them warmly, and offered both a cup of hot chocolate. Once they had their mugs of the steaming liquid in their hand, Barnabas explained the reason for their visit. Kleber surveyed Calvin for a long moment.

"Tall," he said, "Very tall. Dat I must take into account." He disappeared into the back of his shop, and returned minutes later with two long rifles. He held up the weapon with the longer barrel, measuring it against Calvin.

"Dis vun," Kleber said, holding out the gun for Calvin to take. "Dis is de vun for you."

Calvin held the rifle in his hands, admiring the workmanship of the carved wooden stock, the silver patch box, and the unblemished barrel. He placed the rifle butt to his shoulder and sighted down the barrel, surprised at how light and how comfortable the firearm felt. Its balance was remarkable. Kleber grinned with pride.

"A fine rifle," he said. "De man I made it for could not buy it. Lost de money in de faro games." Kleber surveyed Calvin again, satisfied with what he saw. "Dis is de vun for a tall man like you. Please. You must snap it, try with de flint."

Kleber led them through his shop to a small backyard where he had Calvin dry fire the rifle to check its strength of spark. Kleber was pleased with the test—the flint struck the steel cleanly and it was clear that the weapon had been well crafted.

"How much, then, Mr. Kleber?" Barnabas asked. "What is your price for this fine rifle of yours?"

He quoted fourteen dollars. "A fair price, Herr Barnabas. Pay me half now, if you please. Dat's enough for a friend of yours."

"I'll pay you the entire amount," Calvin said. "No need for you to wait for your money." Their trip had consumed less of his funds than he had expected. Between the money in his purse, and the dollars in the money belt he was wearing, Calvin still had an ample reserve, more than enough for the remainder of his trip.

"Dank you," Kleber said, a fresh grin on his face. "Dank you, kindly, sir."

He scurried about his shop pulling together all the additional items Calvin would need: gunpowder, extra bullets and patches, and a spare hickory ramrod. Kleber insisted on making a gift of a fine leather bag to Calvin, and he gave them a few chunks of wood to use for targets.

"Dat should take care of you," he said.

After leaving Kleber's, Barnabas suggested that they test-fire the new rifle. He and Calvin walked together to the outskirts of town and found a vacant field they could use for target practice.

Barnabas placed one of the small blocks of wood Kleber had given them on a large rock and paced off one hundred feet. Calvin busied himself with priming and loading the flintlock. He could tell that Hardwick was watching him, trying to assess how Calvin handled the weapon. It was always that way with men, he thought. They wanted to get your measure, to gauge strengths and weaknesses.

He sighted on the target, and when he was settled, slowly squeezed the trigger. Calvin's first shot missed high and to the right. He reloaded the gun—clumsily he feared—and made the mental adjustment, altering his second shot slightly. He was rewarded with the sight of the ball slamming into the makeshift target, sending the wood block flying.

"Well done," Barnabas said, surprised. "Where did you learn to shoot like that?"

"I'm used to a pistol, not a long rifle, but the idea's the same."

"Can always use a man who is handy with a rifle," Barnabas said. "Helps keep us all in meat, and now's the time to hunt, before the winter fully sets in."

"I'm pleased with Herr Kleber's handiwork. It will suitably impress my New York friends upon my return."

"You'll be a woodsman in no time," Barnabas said. "Dan'l Boone will have a worthy rival."

* * *

They made the trip from Pittsburgh to Cincinnati aboard one of the keelboats that left weekly on its run down the Ohio, carrying passengers, mail, and cargo for the communities scattered along the river. It was some two hundred miles to Cincinnati and with Calvin eager to reach Canaan, traveling by land would take too long. Calvin negotiated his and Barnabas' passage with the captain, one Jarvis Smiley of the keelboat *Janie*.

Calvin was dismayed by the condition of the *Janie*. It was in a sad state, and Calvin could imagine what Seth Elias would have said about its seaworthiness. The crew matched the woeful condition of the boat: the river men were a dirty, rag tag group, poorly dressed, and careless in their approach to their duties. Captain Smiley apparently had given up trying to manage his lackadaisical crew.

Calvin tried not to let his disdain show, although it was hard, accustomed as he was to the more efficient and devoted seamanship practiced by those sailing out of New York. He decided that as long as the *Janie* stayed afloat long enough to bring them to Cincinnati, he would remain silent and be content.

They made slow time. The crew showed interest and energy only when the steersman called them for their ration of corn whiskey, a call that came three times each day (unlike most ocean-going ships, where, wisely, grog was served to the crew only once a day). The result of Captain Smiley's lax policy was a continuously half-drunk group of men barely able to attend to the tasks necessary to sail a watercraft. Smiley kept his demands light, perhaps aware that his men were not predisposed to taking orders in the first place, and so the *Janie* moved down the Ohio in fits and starts.

Calvin spent most of the first leg of their journey, from Pittsburgh to Marietta, reading or surveying the changing landscape on either side of the river. He liked being out on the water again. It made him realize how much he missed the sea. Looking down at the dark waters of the Ohio brought back memories of voyages aboard the *Liberty*, the sense of being free and clear of the petty problems found on shore, of being closer to the elements, of being profoundly attuned to any shifts in the weather and the tides. The Ohio's waters didn't offer the wonderfully changeable colors of the sea, but it was comforting to watch its flow and play, the eddies and currents, as they slipped downstream.

* * *

Captain Smiley had the *Janie* put in at the town of Maysville on the Kentucky side of the Ohio River, where, he announced, they would spend the night. By Calvin's calculations, based on the map of the river that he had purchased in Pittsburgh, they were some seventy miles from Cincinnati.

Calvin was grateful for the break. He had seen enough of Smiley's besotted river men to last a lifetime. The frontier attracted the resourceful and independent, looking for a fresh start, but it also lured the lazy, criminal, and shiftless.

They disembarked at the upper landing, situated just west of Maysville Creek, and made their way past a few warehouses to the main town, which was composed of thirty or forty houses, many of them constructed from logs. There were a few frame houses, a building with a sign proclaiming it the post office, and then a slightly larger structure, the Maysville Inn, which Smiley told them offered the town's best lodging place, because, he explained with a smirk, "seeing as there ain't no other."

Calvin found the innkeeper, a short, poorly shaven man who listened to him indifferently when Calvin asked about lodgings for the night. Barnabas waited a pace behind Calvin.

The innkeeper studied them for a moment, taking in the long rifles each of them carried, their dusty luggage, their dress (Calvin in his coat, breeches, and boots; Hardwick in buckskins).

"You can sleep on the tables down here if you're short of money," the man said. "A pallet in the loft above will cost you more, and the one bed I have left in the backroom will be fifty cents for the night."

"There are two of us," Calvin said.

"The bed's big enough for two."

"That shan't be necessary," Barnabas said to Calvin. "You should take the bed. I can sleep in the loft." He turned to the innkeeper. "How much is that?"

"Twenty-five cents."

"Done," Calvin said. He fished in his leather purse for the money. The innkeeper's mood brightened considerably once he had the coins in his hand.

"Where do you men hail from?" he asked.

"New York," Calvin said, noticing that Barnabas remained silent.

"A long trip, then. How long have you been in Kentucky?"

"Long enough," Barnabas said abruptly, glaring at the innkeeper. Calvin was surprised by his rudeness.

"Mr. Samuels is right to inquire." It was a younger man, slim and well-dressed, who had come up behind them. "There's been trouble with strangers passing through. Theft. Brawling. Drunkenness."

"I disagree," Barnabas said. "I'm under no obligation to explain myself to any man. And who might you be?"

"George Todd," the man said. "A Kentuckian."

"I don't mind answering any questions about our travels, Mr. Todd,"

Calvin said. He didn't care for Todd's arrogant manner, but he saw no point in a confrontation. He introduced himself, and turned to introduce Barnabas, but found that he had already walked away, back towards the inn's entrance. "We're headed to one of the settlements north of Cincinnati."

"You're not dressed like a settler," Todd said. He glanced over Calvin's shoulder, pursing his lips. "Does your friend have a name?"

"That he does," Calvin said. "Barnabas Hardwick."

"Don't recognize it. Yet I feel as though I had seen him somewhere before."

Calvin shrugged. "We're not settlers. I'm from New York, a merchant trader. My companion is living in the Ohio country, a contract hunter for the Army."

Todd motioned for Calvin to take a seat at the table; he sat down himself and called for Mr. Samuels to bring them a jug of apple cider and two mugs.

"I'm here with my wife," Todd said, his tone softening. "We're staying in Maysville for a day or two. She would be pleased to meet a New York gentleman."

Calvin took a sip of the cider. It was potent, and the alcohol swiftly warmed his throat and stomach.

"We've been asking travelers along the river for assistance," Todd said. "Perhaps you can be of help."

"If I can."

"I'm looking for two runaways from our farm. A young girl and a buck, perhaps twenty years old. We think they may be near the river, probably on the Ohio side. Seen any niggers of that description during your journey here?"

Calvin was taken aback. His face must have reflected his disgust, for Todd shifted uneasily.

"It's a question of property," Todd said. "It's no different than someone stealing goods from you. You would want to recover them, and you would have the law on your side."

"One is hardly like the other. I seek no quarrel with you, Mr. Todd, but I agree with Dr. Franklin that slavery represents a debasement of human nature, and should be abolished."

"Yet it is as legal in New York as in Kentucky, is it not? Congress has affirmed that I may retrieve my property, even from another state. It's well known that President Washington had endeavored to recover an escaped slave girl, a maid to his wife, who ran away from Philadelphia and is now in New Hampshire. The law supports the owner in asserting his rights."

"I'm aware of the law. My argument rests on moral, not legal, grounds."

"One man's meat is another man's poison," Todd said. "If you had to deal with the childishness of these people, you would see things differently." Todd squinted as he looked over Calvin's shoulder. "If you will excuse me," he said, and rose from the table and walked to the front door, pausing at the front porch. "Leave those niggers alone, sir," he called out.

From where Calvin was sitting, he could see that Todd was addressing his comments to Barnabas. Calvin rose to his feet and followed Todd to the front door, worried about a possible confrontation between the Kentuckian and Hardwick. At the side of the inn, Barnabas was standing with two black men; he had apparently been talking to them. He turned towards Todd but made no move to leave.

"I told you to stay away from them," Todd said. "Are you deaf?"

"No, I'm not deaf," Barnabas said. "But I talk to anyone I please, when I please."

"You're a damn bold one," Todd said. "Do you seek to provoke me? If so, you won't talk so high and mighty after I've finished thrashing you."

Calvin stepped slightly to the front of Todd, who was glaring at Barnabas, his face flushed and red. The slaves had moved away from Barnabas and were watching from a short distance.

"There's no need for violence," Calvin said, quickly, hoping to forestall trouble. "There's no lasting harm been done here, only some hard words."

"If your rude friend here will apologize...." Todd said, waving a hand dismissively toward Barnabas, a move clearly calculated to provoke him.

"I won't apologize to the likes of you." Barnabas replied, his face contorted with anger, his fists clenched tightly.

Todd gave Calvin an amused look. "Do you see, Mr. Tarkington? I gave your friend his chance to apologize and avoid a thrashing. He didn't take it. He leaves me no recourse. I must teach him some manners."

Calvin shrugged. It was clear that he wasn't going to be able to stop the two younger men from their brawl; they clearly were inclined to fight. He decided he would intervene only if it appeared one was in danger of being badly beaten.

Todd stripped off his waistcoat and stepped out into the dusty street. Barnabas handed his long rifle and hunting bag to Calvin. He stripped his shirt off; he was lean but well-muscled.

"I'm ready for my lesson," he said to Todd, and raised his clenched fists to chest height. Todd wore a confident smile as he put up his own guard.

Todd began to advance towards Barnabas, and then stepped in to throw the first blow, a right hook which Barnabas saw coming and avoided by ducking. He responded with a quick jab to Todd's chin, snapping the Kentuckian's head back. Todd shook his head in anger, the smile gone, and advanced again toward Hardwick.

Barnabas circled away, snapping jabs at Todd when the smaller man moved closer. Calvin could see that Todd was contemplating a rush at Hardwick—perhaps to grab him and wrestle him to the ground. Calvin, who had learned to box when he was a student at Princeton, admired the economy and efficiency of Barnabas' style of fighting.

Todd tried closing on Barnabas quickly, blocking his jab and swinging at his midsection, catching Hardwick with a hard punch to the chest. Barnabas pushed him back with both hands and then caught Todd flush on the chin with an uppercut and followed with a left to the nose. Todd went down hard, blood spurting from his nose, staining his white shirt. Dust rose from the street; Todd sprawled in the dirt.

Barnabas stood, waiting for him. "Had enough?" he asked.

Todd didn't answer. He slowly rose to his feet and brushed the dust off the front of his shirt. He ignored the blood streaming from both nostrils, and put his guard up again. Barnabas followed suit.

Todd changed tactics. He began moving forward slowly, blocking Hardwick's jabs as he went, forcing him back towards the wall of the inn. Calvin could see that Todd hoped to close off any retreat and pin Barnabas against the wall.

Barnabas suddenly moved to the left and launched a hook at Todd's ribs. He connected and Todd, groaning, bent over. That was a mistake: Barnabas threw an uppercut that caught Todd under his chin and jolted his head back violently with the force of the blow.

Todd went down again, hard, onto the ground, rolling over onto his chest. Calvin wasn't sure that the Kentuckian was still conscious. As he lay there, Barnabas stepped forward and kicked Todd hard in the ribs, and would have kicked him again, had Calvin not stepped forward and grabbed his arm, unwilling to countenance any brutality towards a defenseless man.

"That's enough," Calvin said. "Leave him be. He can no longer defend himself."

Barnabas spat on the ground. "It will be a cold day in hell when a slaver teaches me manners."

"Come away," Calvin said, pulling Barnabas by the arm away from the scene. "You more than proved your point."

Todd had begun to stir. Without speaking, Barnabas walked away from Calvin, heading in the direction of the landing.

Todd's slaves came over and helped a stunned Todd to his feet and shepherded their master back into the inn. Calvin could discern no emotion in their faces as they passed him. Todd was staggering slightly, and his eyes were glazed.

Calvin wondered what the slaves were thinking. Did they secretly applaud Barnabas' victory? Or were they loyal to Todd, despite being held in bondage? He had heard apologists for slavery in New York claim that slaves felt like family members, but he had never believed it.

He had been surprised by Barnabas—his sudden anger and resort to violence had exposed a side of this quiet stranger Calvin hadn't seen before. Barnabas seemed to have relished his chance to fight Todd. Calvin had been disturbed when Barnabas had sought to kick Todd when he was down, clearly beaten. It wasn't what he would have expected.

Calvin had learned over the years that the masks that men and women presented to the world obscured their true natures. What did we know of our acquaintances, our neighbors, even our friends? It was easy to misjudge how a man would react to a challenge, to danger, to conflict. Who was Barnabas Hardwick? Calvin couldn't claim to know the man or to answer that question.

SIX

When Calvin returned to the inn, there was no sign of George Todd or his slaves. He made his way to the common room and found Samuels, the innkeeper.

He paid for a mug of cider and decided to wait for Barnabas Hardwick there; he could read and complete some long delayed correspondence in the interim. He needed to be present to head off any trouble if Barnabas returned.

Calvin lost himself in the pages of *Gulliver's Travels* for an hour or so. He took paper, ink, and a quill out of his travel bag so he could write while the room was well-lit. He had brought two quires of paper with him and planned to faithfully keep up with his correspondence with Katharine—even if it would most likely be one-way, for it was unlikely that any mail sent to him would arrive in Cincinnati, the closest town to Canaan with a post office—before he began his return journey.

He sat at the crude, uneven table, and began composing a brief message to Jean Laurent, which he would place inside a longer letter to Katharine.

"May I interrupt you?" a voice asked. Calvin looked up to find an attractive woman standing before him. She was well dressed in an expensive ivory linen dress, and at a glance Calvin could see that her clothing was too fine for a river town like Maysville. Calvin quickly stood up and introduced himself.

She nodded. "I'm Eleanor Todd. You came to my husband's assistance earlier this afternoon. My servants tell me that you prevented him from being beaten any further. You have my thanks."

"Think nothing of it," Calvin said. He noticed that she had called them servants instead of slaves, and that she had a beautiful voice, soft, melodious and precise, with a slight trace of the characteristic Virginia drawl.

"I admire those who act to prevent injustice," she said.

"Then don't admire me," Calvin said. They stood there awkwardly, appraising each other. She was tall, with light brown hair and green eyes and, despite her too prominent nose, an appealing woman. He guessed that she was thirty. "There was no injustice involved. It was a fair fight. I only stepped in when your husband could no longer defend himself."

"George is not used to losing. He prides himself on his skill at boxing. He can be quite hot-tempered. I fear he may have initiated this quarrel."

"The dispute is over. I have counseled Mr. Hardwick to avoid any further trouble, and I would hope that your husband would follow the same course."

"May I sit down, Mr. Tarkington?" she asked.

"Please do," he said, giving her a slight bow. He motioned for her to take the nearest chair, and sat down himself. He folded up his letters and covered them with his copy of *Gulliver's Travels*.

"There's a reason for his temper," she said. "My husband has been suspicious of strangers of late. A month ago two of our servants were kidnapped from our farm. George led a party after them, and one of our men was killed in the pursuit."

"Servants? Do you mean slaves, Mrs. Todd?"

"Slaves, then. In my father's home, in Richmond, they were like part of the family. It's hard for me to think of them as slaves."

"They escaped from your farm?"

"I wouldn't call it an escape. They were enticed with false promises. We know the thieves were white men, and George thinks they may have fled across the river north of here to the Ohio country. We live at Edgemont Hall, some forty miles southwest from here in Kentucky, near Mount Sterling and Winchester."

"You say that a man was killed," Calvin said. "What have the authorities done?"

"What can they do? The killers are somewhere in the Northwest Territory. At a minimum, my husband is determined to find and recover the servants they took. Justice for the murder will be harder, because there were no witnesses, no evidence. The man killed was ambushed."

"It would stand to reason that if you find the slaves, you should find those responsible for the killing," Calvin said.

"Exactly," she said. "That's why George makes inquiries wherever we travel."

She reached into her bag and produced two large wrinkled pieces of paper. She smoothed them out before she handed them to Calvin. They were handbills: the first offered a $100 reward for information leading to the capture of a female slave, Flavia, described as a light-skinned Negro girl of fifteen years. The second handbill described a male runaway, Cicero, a slave of twenty years with a "T" brand on his cheek, with a reward of $50.

Calvin was surprised at the size of the rewards offered, particularly for the girl. He had seen advertisements in the *New-York Gazette* with bounties of $20 or so for the recovery of runaways (and had been disgusted by them). He wondered why the reward for the girl was so high.

"These are large rewards," he said. "They must be highly prized by your husband to offer such amounts."

"They are." She looked away from him and didn't offer a further explanation.

"What would motivate men to come to your farm for these slaves? To take such risks?"

"You would have to ask them," she said coolly in her beautiful voice. "Why are there horse thieves? Why do men covet their neighbor's goods?" She paused. "Their wives?"

"Common thieves steal for financial gain. The motives of the men who helped your slaves to escape had to be quite different. Were they abolitionists? If they sought to free these slaves, they could enjoy no financial benefit from their actions. In fact, they risked their own lives and property on principle, however misguided their methods."

"You find their methods misguided, but you approve of their principles?"

"I'll not disguise that fact, Mrs. Todd," he said. "I told your husband my views earlier. Slavery is a barbaric and cruel institution. It degrades all those involved in it. It should be abolished in this country. Through legal means, of course."

She flushed. He imagined that she was not used to hearing slavery condemned in so straightforward a manner. "If you had grown up with these people, you would understand. They're childish and naturally lazy. They need discipline. They're part of an inferior race. Surely you won't dispute that? Or are you prepared to invite them into your home? Marry your children? I doubt that, sir."

It was his turn to flush at her sarcasm.

"I believe that no man should be held in bondage," he said. "Whether I count him as my equal or not. But I have no wish to quarrel with you, ma'am. There's been enough of that already for today."

"Then we must turn to other topics," she said with a nervous smile. "Tell me of your plans: are you are looking to settle here? Across the river, then? In the Symmes Purchase or the Virginia Military District?"

"I'm only a sojourner. I'm here to visit a friend in the Ohio country. I have a wife waiting for me in New York."

"Quite a long journey to undertake to see a friend."

"I'm accustomed to traveling considerable distances," Calvin replied. "By ship, however, not by horse or carriage. My friend requested my assistance, and he would have not sought my presence unless it was needed. So, here I am."

"You have seen the world, then," she said. "I envy you. I have read of life in London and Paris and the great cities. I've wondered what they might be like."

"Crammed with all man can imagine and devise for his comfort and pleasure," Calvin said. "Filled with men and women of all walks, the rich and the poor. Theaters, shops, taverns, dance halls, parks, elegant residences, and royal palaces. Mr. Johnson has said that when a man is tired of London, he is tired of life. Nonetheless, I prefer New York. We have many of the advantages, but fewer of the disadvantages, of these large cities. And we have the harbor, and the ocean beyond."

"I've seen the ocean once," she said. "As a child, in Virginia. It was so vast."

They were interrupted by the appearance of George Todd in the doorway. He limped over to the table, and Calvin could smell the alcohol on his breath. Todd's face was bruised, and there was an ugly welt under his eye.

"I understand that thanks are owed," he said to Calvin. "For your intervention."

Calvin shook his head. "As I told your wife, I simply wanted it to remain a fair fight."

"I underestimated your friend," Todd said, his words slightly slurred. "I won't make that mistake again."

"There's no call for any further trouble," Calvin said. "We will leave in the morning for Cincinnati."

"Mr. Tarkington is from New York," Eleanor Todd said quickly. "I've learned that he's quite a traveler."

"There's not much to see in Maysville," Todd said. "A miserable town." He fixed his eyes on Calvin. "I regret that this is how we've made our acquaintance. Damned if I don't lose my temper at the most inopportune times."

"That's in the past, now," Calvin said.

"Should you ever find yourself near Winchester, you must stop by Edgemont Hall," Todd said. "We would be honored to host you."

Calvin rose to his feet, eager to finish the conversation. "Thank you. I plan to return home by the New Year, so I'll have to decline your invitation." He collected his papers and book, and turned to Eleanor. "A pleasure to meet you, ma'am." He gave them a short bow, and left.

* * *

Calvin found Barnabas standing on the dock next to the *Janie* staring out across the river. When Calvin touched his shoulder, Barnabas turned to face him.

"I make no apologies," Barnabas said, gazing back at the river. A brisk wind was ruffling the surface of the dark water.

"I ask for none. I'm curious. What was the nature of your conversation with Todd's slaves?"

"It was straight-forward," he said. "I asked them if they knew they could be free on the other side of the river." He motioned across the Ohio. "In the Northwest Territory."

"If Todd had overheard that, he could have the law on you."

"I respect no law that robs a man of his freedom, or constrains him from encouraging others to seize theirs."

"That's your right," Calvin said. "The law can be harsh for those who flout it."

Barnabas spat into the water below. "I had heard of George Todd of Kentucky before today. He mistreats his slaves. He deserves the beating I gave him today."

"You surprise me," Calvin said. "I did not anticipate that you would hold such strong feelings on the question."

"I was raised among the Friends in Pennsylvania. There never was any question that slavery was an abomination."

"Did you learn how to fight from the Quakers?" Calvin asked with a slight smile.

"I don't believe in turning the other cheek," Barnabas said quietly. "If you hit me, I'll hit you back twice as hard. That philosophy has served me well. As to slavery, I've learned more since I've been here. You will encounter freed men and runaways on our side of the river. They are property, slaves, in Kentucky, but if they can cross the Ohio River, then they have a chance for freedom. Some are living with the Shawnee and Delaware, some by themselves, some in settlements with whites."

"Are they truly free?" Calvin asked. "There's no safe harbor for them in Ohio, is there? What of the Fugitive Act? Is it not a crime to help or shelter a runaway?"

"A bad law many choose to ignore."

"A law nonetheless," Calvin said. "What would the world come to if we only observed those laws we preferred?"

"You worry too much about the law. What should matter is what we know is right. Judah agrees with me. Most of us in the Territory feel the same." He frowned. "I'll sleep on the boat tonight. I wouldn't trust myself if I saw that bastard Todd again."

SEVEN

They arrived in Cincinnati at one o'clock on a warm, lazy October afternoon, almost two months to the day since their departure from New York.

As the *Janie* had moved down the Ohio and closer to the docks at Cincinnati, the crew began preparing the ship to land, displaying more alacrity than at any other time during the journey. They were all eager to reach Cincinnati, Calvin thought, most likely because of the taverns there. A slight breeze blew from the southeast across the surface of the river, and Calvin enjoyed the feel of the sun warming his face. He positioned himself near the front of the boat so he could survey the town. Barnabas came over and joined him.

"We've come a fair distance," he said. "It won't be long now before we reach Judah. Canaan's three or four days ride from Cincinnati."

They were interrupted by the sound of Captain Smiley roundly cursing the crewman stationed at the tiller, concerned that the *Janie* might collide with the dock at the landing. The pilot reacted, shifting the boat's course as it headed towards shore, and easing it toward the dock. There was a light bump and several of the crew jumped onto the dock and began securing the *Janie* with short lines.

Cincinnati had been built on two tiered banks fronting the river, the first touching the Ohio, where flatboats, barges, keelboats, and pirogues crowded the landing, and the next sloping up to the hills that surrounded the town. Cincinnati proper—if the town merited a separate and distinct status, Calvin thought—was composed of a hundred or so frame buildings, most of them clustered on the first bank, near the waterfront.

It was the official seat of government for the Northwest Territory and the only town of any size in the region, but it was an unprepossessing place, distinguished only by its location, near the mouth of two rivers, and having little appeal to the eye.

Calvin looked up from the landing to the log palisades of Fort Washington perched on a promontory above, part of the small range of hills that wrapped around the town. A small, bedraggled American flag with sixteen stars stitched on the blue field for each of the new Republic's states, hung limply from an oak pole.

General Anthony Wayne had employed Cincinnati as his staging ground in his successful campaign to subdue the Shawnee. It had been a brutal struggle, with no quarter given, the Americans determined to avenge the defeat of the feckless Arthur St. Clair and his troops on the banks of the Wabash River. There had been atrocities on both sides, Calvin knew, and the settlers along the Ohio had welcomed the great victory at Fallen Timbers in 1794 and the ensuing Peace of Greenville the following year, which promised a respite from the threat of concerted Indian hostilities.

It had been quiet since then, with an occasional renegade Shawnee, Mingo, or Wyandot band striking at an isolated farm or settlement, but most of the Indians had retreated further west, moving their villages into western Ohio and beyond.

Barnabas tugged on Calvin's arm and pointed skyward.

"A red hawk," he said.

They stood at the side of boat in silence admiring the hawk, its broad wingspan evident even from quite a distance, as it soared on the wind above the fort, wheeling around in the air. The hawk turned and floated towards the river, drawing Calvin's attention east to Kentucky, to the mouth of the Licking River and the small town of Newport.

They planned to make their stop in Cincinnati brief. At the landing below the main section of the town, Calvin and Barnabas bid farewell to Captain Smiley. He had apparently heard stories from the crew of Hardwick's fistfight with George Todd in Maysville and now regarded Barnabas much more favorably. The captain was in a mood to talk.

"Don't let any of the roustabouts provoke you," Smiley advised Barnabas. "Can't be settling all differences with your fists."

Barnabas slapped Smiley on the back. "I'll take your advice to heart."

"So keep a sharp eye out for troublemakers," the captain continued. "You know the type. There are a fair number of soldiers in town because of the fort. They're trouble when they've been drinkin', especially the veterans. Watch for them."

"I shall try, Captain," Barnabas said, grinning. "I hope to avoid any further disputes."

"A wise course, Barnabas. A prudent one. Now concerning this fracas in Maysville, is it true that you left the other, ah, gentleman in the street, face down, badly battered?"

"Don't believe all the stories you hear."

"Were you there, Mr. Tarkington?" Smiley asked Calvin. "At this fracas? What sort was it? Rough and ready, or more gentleman-like?"

"It's hard to be a judge of that," Calvin said, enjoying the absurdity of the conversation, trying not to laugh out loud. "It depends on your perspective. Was it gentlemanly? For the most part. No gouging or biting."

"Wish I could have seen it," Smiley said wistfully. "Always enjoyed watching a rough-and-tumble with men who know how to handle themselves. Had I known in advance, you can be damn sure that I'd have been there."

"It's been my experience that those observing the battle enjoy it more than those fighting," Calvin said, and Barnabas laughed. "Certainly, the outcome is of less importance to the spectator. They don't suffer the bruises and broken bones. As long as there's some action, they're satisfied."

Smiley didn't take offense. "I only wish I were a tad bit younger," he said. "I think I could have given you a go, then, Barnabas, when I was in my prime. Bare knuckles are for a younger man. You don't heal up as well as you get older."

"Then I'm fortunate that you're a mature man, Captain," Barnabas said. "It allows us to part now as friends, none the worse for wear."

Captain Smiley grinned and pumped their hands. Calvin paid him the last of their fare in silver dollars, which made Smiley's grin grow wider.

Once on shore, Calvin could not get much of a feel for Cincinnati and its small cluster of wood-framed buildings and muddy streets. It existed, he thought, only because its location near the mouth of two other rivers, the Licking River in Kentucky and the Miami in Ohio, which had made it an ideal spot for the fort and then as a trading post.

They made their way to Burt & Newman's Saddlery, and bargained with Mr. Burt for the rental of two saddle horses, a sorrel mare and a large bay horse, for the final leg of the journey, promising to return the mounts within the week. Then they went over to Jones' Dry Goods store and purchased salt, flour, coffee, dried beans, and gunpowder, all basic provisions in demand on the frontier.

Calvin took a detour to the printer's shop, run by a relative newcomer to Cincinnati named Joseph Carpenter (who edited the town's weekly newspaper, the *Western Spy and Hamilton Gazette*) where he purchased a recently published map of the Northwest Territory. Carpenter tried to sell him a copy of a tract entitled "Observations on the Alien and Sedition Laws," but Calvin politely declined. He didn't need to be convinced of the unfairness of the Acts; it was clear to him that President Adams and the Federalists sought to suppress the Republican press with the legislation.

If Livingston Rhodes had been there, he could have launched into a long tirade against the Hamiltonians and their motives. Livingston had adopted the repeal of the Acts as a personal crusade, railing against them in the New York newspapers aligned with Mr. Jefferson and his party, and producing his own inflammatory pamphlets.

"Soon I'll be printing a new pamphlet about President Adams and tyranny," Carpenter said. "Written by Dr. O'Shea, a fellow newcomer to Cincinnati."

"A doctor of medicine?" Calvin asked.

"A physic trained in England, they say. He's on the east side of town. A good reputation. Doesn't drink to excess. We don't see too many doctors this far west. I reckon he's as good as you're going to git."

"We should stop by and meet this doctor," Calvin said. "For Judah."

Barnabas nodded. "It can't hurt."

A passerby directed them to East Street. An elegant hand-painted sign on the outside of a gray frame house proclaimed that it was the residence of *Doctor John O'Shea, lately of Dublin, Ireland, physick and surgeon.* A striking rendering of the staff of Asclepius—a serpent encircling a long staff—with a green shamrock next to it, decorated the bottom half of the sign. Calvin and Barnabas stood for a moment admiring the sign, surprised to find such an artistic creation on a Cincinnati street.

The front door was unlocked, and after knocking, Calvin heard a deep male voice calling out for him to "enter," and so he led the way deeper into the house. There was no sign of any patients waiting to see O'Shea.

In a large room adjacent to a cramped kitchen, they found O'Shea seated at a rough wooden table in front of a chessboard, peering intently at the pieces. The room was sparsely furnished with crude furniture. Large leather-bound medical books filled the top shelf of a wooden bookcase, the other shelves were empty.

A balding, middle-aged man with a ruddy face and wide-set eyes, O'Shea gave the appearance, Calvin decided, of being slightly surprised. He blinked a few times rapidly when Calvin and Barnabas introduced themselves. Calvin noticed that there were toast crumbs clinging to his stained waistcoat.

O'Shea slowly, and reluctantly, turned to face them. It was clear that he did not care for his game being interrupted by their arrival.

"It's my turn," he explained. Calvin noticed that he had a slight brogue. "My opponent, Mr. Williams, had a pressing errand to run. He's left me in a precarious situation, with my queen under imminent threat." He sighed and stood up. "What may I do for you gentlemen?

"You are a doctor of medicine," Calvin said, making it more of a statement than a question, although O'Shea's dishevelment and his reluctance to abandon the chessboard did not bode well in Calvin's view.

"I'm a doctor of medicine," O'Shea said. "The only London-trained physic within four hundred miles, I would wager."

"You have quite the sign outside."

"Indeed. Fashioned for me in Philadelphia by Mr. Mathew Pratt. A fine painter, known for his portraits when he went to London and studied with Benjamin West, but he couldn't make a living in America as an artist. So he paints signs." He grinned, and Calvin had the feeling he had told the story of Matthew Pratt many times. "What need did you have for a doctor?"

"Neither of us do," Calvin explained. "It's a friend." He turned to Barnabas. "Can you describe Judah's symptoms?"

"Pain in the belly. He has lost weight. He says he has little appetite." Barnabas paused. "He looks ill. His skin has a yellowish cast."

"It could be many things," O'Shea said. "It could be jaundice, *morbus regius*, the king's disease, or something more serious. Can he come here so I can examine him?"

Calvin and Barnabas exchanged glances. "We'll see," Calvin said. "Our friend had hoped to see Dr. Rush in Philadelphia."

"Dr. Benjamin Rush? All the way to Philadelphia? Certainly no need for that with Dr. Jack O'Shea at your beck and call."

Calvin nodded. "You're confident, Dr. O'Shea, and that's a quality one would hope to find in a physician. You may see us again, with our friend, for your expert diagnosis."

"Does your friend play chess?" O'Shea asked. "If he'll play a game or two, I'll offer him my lowest rates for a consultation. You have no idea how hard it is to find chess players here in this wilderness."

* * *

They decided not to stay the night, but instead to begin their trip to

Canaan. As they followed the trail through the hills above Cincinnati, Calvin looked back at the river below them. Living in New York, seeing the harbor nearly every day, he had grown accustomed to being around open water. He knew it was somewhat irrational, but he disliked being distant from the sea.

Barnabas set a brisk pace from the start. He was eager to reach Canaan, and he had them pause only briefly to rest the horses and eat.

There were few signs of human habitation on the trip, only a few lean-tos and scattered cabins of settlers along the way. It served to make Calvin more aware of the rawness, the newness of the country, and more conscious of its isolation.

Twice they came across massive raised mounds. Calvin had read that the Indian burial mounds dotted the territory, and so he was not surprised by them. He noticed that Barnabas gave them a wide berth and did not care to linger too long in their vicinity. Calvin was not by nature a superstitious man, and he was surprised to find that the mounds made Barnabas uneasy.

"I wouldn't walk over a grave in a cemetery, and this is no different," he explained when Calvin asked. "No call to stir up the past."

The solitude of the forest was different than that of the sea. The dense canopy of hardwood trees overhead served to cut off any view of the sky; at sea, Calvin was always conscious of the firmament above and around him, open to view, sometimes merging with the water at the horizon line. Once into the forest, there was a closeness, a sense of surrounding, enveloping darkness, that he had never experienced on the open sea when sailing, even at night.

Calvin wondered how long it would take for the inexorable movement of newcomers, of immigrants and the restless, to thin the great forest around them and occupy the land. Two generations? Three? Perhaps sooner if the war continued in Europe—driving that troubled continent's refugees and exiles to America—and the economy in New York and Philadelphia worsened because of the war's dampening effect on trade. Men without work were more likely to head west for the promise of cheap land and a chance for a fresh start. With luck, and dogged perseverance, some of the settlers would prosper and build new towns and cities.

On the morning of the second day, they stopped on a ridge and looked down onto a broad expanse dotted with what at first glance appeared to be cattle. When Calvin focused for a long moment, he realized that they were shaggy-haired buffaloes. Calvin had seen the animals before in New York, exhibited as a curiosity, but not a herd of the creatures in the wild.

"First time that you have encountered buffalo?" Barnabas asked. "A smallish herd. They used to be much more common. Hunted over, I'm afraid."

"They are strange looking creatures," Calvin said. "I've seen a few in New York, at an exhibition, where I also saw an elephant."

"An elephant?" Barnabas was amused by the thought. "That must have been something."

"Brought from India by a Salem shipmaster, Jacob Crowninshield." It was not the only time Calvin had encountered an elephant. He remembered seeing the Emperor Ch'ien-lung's elephants being paraded through the narrow streets of Peking, the capital city of the Celestial Empire.

"We won't stop to take any," Barnabas said, surveying the buffalo below them. "Though I am tempted. Fresh meat is always a welcome commodity in Canaan."

They rode on and camped that night on the other side of the valley where they had seen the buffalo.

On the fourth day, as they neared the Miami River, Calvin was moved by the beauty of the vivid oranges, reds, and browns in the landscape around them, the changing leaves of the massive oaks, hickories, chestnuts, and other trees of the yet untamed Ohio forest, interspersed with the bluish green boughs of the pines and other conifers. He may have missed the fall in New York, he thought, but the brilliant colors and crisp weather he had encountered partially made up for it.

He breathed in deeply the smell of the wet leaves already on the ground—a sweet, tangy odor—bringing back memories of his childhood, playing in the fields of his grandfather's farm, the taste of autumn cider, of roasted pumpkin and chestnuts. The Tarkington land in western

Massachusetts had once been part of the wilderness, too, at least from the settlers' viewpoint, occupied only by scattered bands of Indians. Now it was as placid and calm as Surrey or Kent in England.

As they neared Canaan, they had to wade through a few streams, branches of the Miami River, leading their horses by their bridles. Barnabas explained that Canaan was a scattering of homesteads, crude log cabins in rough clearings, connected by trails.

They passed one such clearing, but Barnabas kept riding, unwilling to delay their arrival. They stopped briefly at Barnabas's rough cabin, which was located at the southernmost edge of the dwellings and closest to the river.

His log house had been recently constructed. There were open chinks between the logs—Barnabas hadn't yet bothered to fill them with mud, he explained—and a portion of the roof had not been completed. He planned to finish the work on his dwelling later in the fall, before the colder weather of December. He would ask for help from Judah and some of his other neighbors and they would finish the roof in a day's work.

Inside the cabin, Barnabas had a rudimentary fireplace with a spit and a single bronze pot, a roughly constructed table, two chairs, and a pallet. He threw his satchel on the pallet.

"Judah will want you to stay with him," he said. "His cabin has more room and a few more comforts. He put a lot more effort into making it livable. He had Rachel and Naomi to think of."

Barnabas explained that they had worked together to clear the land, cutting down the massive trees and burning the stumps in what was called the New England method. The settlers from Virginia and the Carolinas did not expend the same effort. They preferred to girdle the trees, slowly killing them, and then planting around them. Settlers from New England, used to stony fields and exhausted soil, had been delighted by the rich loam of the Ohio Valley. It made good farmland—crops flourished, and the yield from an acre greatly surpassed their expectations.

They rode a few miles and came to another clearing and a large cabin with a field of sorts, littered with occasional tree stumps but planted with irregular rows of Indian corn. They tethered their horses and advanced on foot towards a somewhat larger log house which had a porch, of sorts, at its front. There was a thin trail of smoke coming from its crude, short chimney. Calvin wondered, for a moment, what it would be like to live there for any extended period of time, to be so isolated, to have the clearing and the forest around it become the boundaries of one's world.

"Judah's place," Barnabas said. They dismounted, and he hailed the house, loudly calling out Judah's name several times, and the door to the cabin swung open to reveal a slim figure, dressed in buckskins like Barnabas, with dark hair tied in a queue, and a gaunt, but handsome, face.

Calvin reached the porch in a few strides and embraced Judah. He was surprised at how lean his friend was; Judah had always been solidly well proportioned. As he embraced him, Calvin could feel how bony Judah had become under his rough clothing.

Judah looked tired and held himself stiffly. His face had a sallow cast and Calvin was dismayed at how sickly his once vital friend had become. As harsh as life on the frontier could be, it would not explain Judah's deterioration. Calvin studied Judah's lean face carefully, looking for clues to the nature of his illness.

Calvin was silent for a moment. "I'm glad to see you," he said. "Much has happened since we were last together."

"That it has," Judah said. "I was heartsick to learn of Sarah's passing."

Calvin stopped. There wasn't anything more to say; he knew Judah would understand. They had been rivals, once. They had both courted Sarah that summer in Paris, each hoping for her hand in marriage; she had chosen Calvin, the outsider, a stranger, over Judah, the safe choice, the suitor preferred by her father.

To his credit, Judah had accepted her decision without complaint or resentment. Placing himself in danger, he had helped Calvin leave Paris and make his way to Spain when the Jacobin authorities of the Commune had been searching for him. Their escape from Paris had gone badly and in a confrontation outside the barrier, Calvin had been forced to shoot and kill a Jacobin investigator, Judah's superior, to protect

Judah and himself. They were not memories that Calvin particularly wanted to dwell on.

"Come meet Rachel," Judah said. "And my daughter, Naomi."

Rachel was a slim, nervous woman who welcomed Calvin and Barnabas with a smile. Naomi hid in her mother's skirts, poking her face out once or twice to spy on Calvin and to grin at Barnabas.

"You must eat," Rachel said and led them into the cabin, which smelled of wood smoke. Calvin could see that she was curious about him—she kept stealing glances over at him as he bustled about the crude kitchen.

They made small talk as she prepared their meal: venison stew, cornmeal cakes, and beans. Calvin could feel his hunger growing as the savory smell of the cooking filled the cabin. Then they sat together at the puncheon table and ate their fill. Judah did not eat much, Calvin noticed, picking at his food.

When they were finished with the meal, Barnabas took his leave. Calvin and Judah sat side-by-side on the small front porch and talked.

"Thank you for coming all this way," Judah began. "It is no small thing."

Calvin shook his head. "Not for a friend."

"Soon it will be too cold for Rachel and Naomi to travel. I'm relieved that you will accompany us on the journey. That is, should anything happen to me."

"We met a doctor in Cincinnati," Calvin said. "London-trained. Perhaps you should see him. It's a lot closer than Philadelphia."

"We must travel east whether or not my health improves," Judah said. "We cannot stay here. It's not safe for us."

"I don't understand."

"Rachel's father, Daniel Flint, founded Canaan. He's an abolitionist, a fierce one. He has provided sanctuary for escaped slaves in his home. It is only a matter of time before the slave catchers come here. I fear what will happen then."

"He's on the wrong side of the law with this. It's madness on his part."

"Men make laws," Judah said. "If those laws violate the principles of liberty and equality, then I say they are illegitimate. I'm proud that we banned slavery in France."

"We cannot live without laws," Calvin said. He didn't want to argue with Judah, but he couldn't stay silent. "Nor should we pick and choose the ones we obey. There are consequences for that."

"I'm aware of those consequences," Judah said. "I'm willing to risk them, but I won't place Rachel and Naomi in harm's way. It's as simple as that."

"I understand," Calvin said. "In fact, I have a wife waiting for me in New York. We've been married for a few months, and I have come to appreciate how close the bonds of matrimony can be."

"That's gladdening news. And her name?"

"Katharine. She's Irish, and you would approve of her politics. She has a mind of her own. But you will learn that for yourself, because I will insist that you and your family come to New York."

EIGHT

New York

That Friday morning Katharine realized, with a growing certainty, that she was with child. She felt sick to her stomach when she awoke, and when she left her bed, she was slightly dizzy. She had missed her period twice, and she had been gaining weight for the past few weeks. Katharine touched her stomach, mindful of the life that she now carried.

She secretly had wondered if she could get pregnant. She and Sean had slept together for years without making a child. Now, after only a few months, she was carrying Calvin's baby. What would it be like to have a third person in their lives, while they were still getting to know each other? She hoped it would bring them closer together.

Now that she was certain, she would share the news with Calvin in a letter. Before they left for the frontier, Barnabas Hardwick has suggested that she send any letters to Calvin at Griffin Yeatman's Tavern in Cincinnati. While there was no guarantee that Calvin would receive the letter, she wanted to try nonetheless.

She trusted that Calvin would back in New York by Christmas, and so there would be time for him to adjust to her altered condition. She counted herself as lucky. She knew that wives of sea captains might give birth to a child when their husbands were thousands of miles distant. It might be a year or more before a father set eyes on his son or daughter.

She didn't think that she would be showing for several more weeks—one of the benefits of being tall—but she would have to alter her dresses to accommodate her growing belly.

She fought back her worries, telling herself that she shouldn't succumb to the dark pessimism that it seemed was the birthright of the Irish. She had met a wonderful man and married him, and now she would bear his child, and it shouldn't follow that her good fortune would be inevitably followed by a reversal of that fortune.

She had resigned herself to the fact that seeing Judah would bring back memories for Calvin of Sarah. She didn't like that, but in the end Calvin would return to New York, and to their shared life, and she was certain that she would have him back again, hers.

* * *

Livingston Rhodes arrived just after lunch on Saturday. Katharine suspected that Calvin had asked him to stop by at least once a week, although Livingston denied it when she asked. She enjoyed seeing him—he always related the latest news and then had a humorous story or two to tell.

She asked Livingston to take a walk with her. She was eager to get outside. It was one of those surprisingly warm days, a gift to New Yorkers so late in autumn. The streets were filled with people enjoying the weather.

They took the carriage to Bowling Green, and entered the park through the open gate. They strolled through the park, Katharine enjoying the touch of the sun on her face.

Livingston glanced over to the center of the park, where there was an empty marble pedestal. "I'll never forget the day the statue of King George came down," he said. "Another sign that there was no turning back for us. The Sons of Liberty were determined to destroy any vestiges of royal rule. They even sawed off the crowns on the wrought-iron fence."

"Perhaps someday we'll be able to say the same thing about royal rule in Dublin," she said.

"Do you think about the struggle there much?" Livingston asked.

"I still care about what happens in Ireland, but my life is here, now." She took a deep breath. "I have exciting news. I'm with child. It will become quite apparent before Calvin returns, so he may be the last in New York to know."

"Wonderful," Livingston said, a smile spreading across his face. "Calvin will be delighted. When do you expect the birth?"

"In the spring. Please don't say anything, yet. I've written to Calvin telling him."

"My lips are sealed," Livingston said.

She noticed a man walking toward them. There was something familiar about him, but she couldn't immediately recall where she might have encountered him.

"I'll be damned," he said loudly. "Kate Connaughton. In the flesh."

At the sound of his voice, she remembered him—Devlin Phelan, a member of Theobald Wolfe Tone's circle in Dublin. She had taken an immediate dislike to Phelan—he was arrogant and vain. She had caught him boldly staring at her more than once when Sean wasn't with her.

"Kate," Phelan said. "Never thought I'd find you here, in New York."

"It's Katharine Tarkington these days," she said, immediately ill-at-ease. "I have remarried." She paused, trying to collect her thoughts. "Mr. Phelan, this is Mr. Rhodes, a friend of my husband."

"I've heard of you," Phelan said, nodding to Livingston. "You've taken up the pen in support of the Irish cause in the newspapers here."

"That I have," Livingston said. "Ireland should be free."

"I long for that day. I only wish I was there instead of here. We've been plagued by traitors, you know. Martial law since March. Lord Edward Fitzgerald betrayed to the British in May. Informers have been swarming to the Castle to tell our secrets."

"How long have you been in New York?" Katharine asked.

"A few weeks," Phelan said. "I came under suspicion myself, and I'm lucky to have gotten out with my own skin. I'm sorry about Sean. I've no doubt that he fought the bastards to the very last."

"Thank you," she replied. "It was a shock to lose him."

"You've married since," Phelan said, with a slight smile that Katharine didn't like.

She felt herself tense as he stared at her in a challenging way. "Quite recently," she said.

"I'd like to meet the lucky man who swept Kate Connaughton off her feet."

"There's none finer," Livingston said. "Calvin Tarkington is a gentleman of quality."

"Is he now?" Phelan said, and Katharine caught the edge in his voice, even if Livingston didn't. "That's a grand thing—that Kate has landed a gentleman of quality."

"There's no question of that," Livingston said. "And Calvin has been fortunate to find such a wife. We were beginning to think he'd never marry. Katharine changed his mind."

"I'm sure she did."

"We won't keep you, Mr. Phelan," Katharine said, hoping to conclude the conversation as quickly as she could.

"Mr. Phelan?" He smirked. "My name is still Devlin."

"I shall remember that," she said. "If you will excuse us, Mr. Rhodes and I have an appointment we must keep."

"A pleasure meeting you," Livingston said to Phelan.

"Ah, but we have much to discuss," Phelan said, staring at Katharine. "There are a few of us here in New York raising support for the cause. When can I call upon you, Kate?"

"Where are you staying?" she asked. "I can send a message when it's convenient for you to visit." She silently resolved that it would never be convenient for her to receive Devlin Phelan.

He shrugged. "No need," he said. "I'm sure I can find my way to the home of the illustrious Calvin Tarkington."

Phelan gave them a short bow, and walked away, heading north.

"There's something unpleasant about that man's manner," Livingston said.

"I never cared for him," she said. "Nor did Sean. I would hope that I don't see him again, and if he comes calling I won't receive him."

"Are you all right?"

"I'm fine. It was a bit of a shock to meet Phelan here. He didn't come to America with Mr. Tone when Sean and I did."

She wished she could share with Livingston why encountering Phelan had so unsettled her, but she could not. How could she tell her husband's best friend that she was a liar? That, despite what Calvin believed, she and Sean had never married, and she was not a widow.

While it was true that they had been seen as man-and-wife by friend and family, there had been no marriage ceremony, religious or civil. No posting of banns. No marriage license. From a legal perspective, Katharine might be considered Sean Daly's common law wife, but that was not how Calvin understood her past marital status.

Katharine believed that for all intents and purposes she *had* been married to Sean—sharing his bed, sharing his good and bad fortune (mostly bad), remaining faithful to him (even if he had strayed). It did not matter, in one sense, how their relationship was defined, but yet it made a huge difference.

She was ashamed, not for "living in sin" with Sean, but for not having the courage to tell Calvin the truth before their marriage. She hadn't wanted to alter the way that he perceived her. She also knew that for Calvin to marry a widow was one thing—to marry the mistress of another man was another. Would he feel that she had deliberately misled him?

It was bad luck that Phelan had found his way to New York when he did. There were only a few in Dublin who had known the truth about Sean and her, and Phelan was one.

"Shall we continue our walk?" Livingston asked, bringing her back to the present.

"By all means," she said. "We must catch our sunshine where we may."

* * *

Katharine didn't have to wait long to learn that Devlin Phelan hadn't been deterred by his less-than-enthusiastic reception at Bowling Green. On Monday, she found him at her front door, wearing the same sly smile on his face.

"I thought I'd call upon you," he said. He looked past her into the house. "Are you going to invite me in? Your friend from the past?"

"Were we friends?" she asked.

"We could have been good friends, Kate. We never got the chance. My loss, of course."

She was annoyed that he had continued to call her Kate.

"My husband is not here at the moment," she said.

"No, he's not, is he? They say he's off to the frontier. I've asked around. He's a wealthy one, Mr. Calvin Tarkington. You've done well, but you've always had an eye for the main chance, haven't you?"

"Did you come here to insult me?"

"I mean to compliment you," he said. "On your cleverness. They say you came here as Mrs. Katharine Daly, 'cept you and I both know that you were no more married to Sean than I am to Lady Hamilton."

"I don't see how that is your business."

"As an old friend, you can trust me to keep your secrets. Friends help each other.

"I don't need your help," she said.

"But *your* assistance is needed. You're a woman of means, now, and those of us who have sacrificed for the cause of Ireland need support."

"Support?"

"Financial support. Until we can get back on our feet."

"Are you asking for money?" She stared directly at him—it was her turn to give a challenging look.

"You're asking for my silence on certain matters. I think it's a fair exchange."

"An exchange? I want nothing from you."

"Do you wish all of New York to know about your past, Kate? I think not."

He caught her by surprise, grabbing her by the shoulders and giving her a hard kiss on the lips. She twisted away from him, furious, and slapped him in the face.

"You bastard," she said, reddening. "How dare you."

"You're quite fetching when you blush," he said.

She pushed the door shut in his face and bolted it. Her heart beat rapidly, and she tried to calm herself.

"I'll be back," Phelan said. She could hear his voice clearly through the door. "I want you to think about what I've said. About keeping your reputation spotless. I expect you to be in a more giving mood when we meet next. I think twenty Spanish silver dollars to start would demonstrate your good faith."

She said nothing in reply, stationing herself by the window where she could watch the street without being seen. She watched Phelan stride up Greenwich Street, exuding confidence, and she hated him and his sudden, uninvited appearance in her life.

It wasn't just that he could damage her good name by spreading stories—she knew there would be some in New York who would delight in learning that Mrs. Calvin Tarkington had a checkered past. Phelan had made her conscious of how vulnerable she was, living in the house by herself.

She went to the drawing room fireplace and found the wrought-iron poker. She felt the heft of the metal pole in her hand. She placed it by the front door, where it would be nearby if Phelan decided to return, and she had to defend herself. She shivered at the thought. She would need to take further measures for her safety, and she couldn't afford any delays.

PART THREE

NINE

The Northwest Territory

The meeting takes place at the landing, where the Great River bottoms and gradually becomes shallow at its southern edge. A slight breeze stirs the ovate golden-yellow leaves of the birch trees by the water. It is late in the afternoon, yet the sun remains strong enough to shine brightly, intensely, on the river surface. The glare blinds the two men waiting on the riverbank; they do not see the canoe until it is within some two hundred yards of the shoreline.

Two Shawnee of the Piqua clan effortlessly paddle the canoe towards the shore. The canoe glides smoothly through the water, propelled by their rhythmic efforts, moving quietly enough that its arrival surprises several geese by the riverside, who escape, startled, honking, wings flapping. The Indians beach their craft expertly on the shore, and then drag it several feet onto the bank. Large oak trees on both sides screen the landing, north and south: the foliage ensures that this meeting will remain unobserved.

The larger of the two Shawnee approaches the waiting men. His companion remains by the canoe, a flintlock rifle in hand.

The Shawnee moves with a slow, unhurried stride. A big man, he is well muscled under his worn and stained fringed hunting shirt. He wears a dark brown headband, a nose ring, and ear bobs suspended from ear lobes that have been split in the Shawnee fashion. His face, reddish-brown from the sun, is hairless and smooth. He carries a tomahawk in one hand, loosely. He stops a few feet away, and exchanges greetings with the two men.

The white men are a mismatched pair. One is slim and fashionably dressed in breeches and a green coat; the other, short and heavy-set, wears buckskins and appears to be somewhat ill at ease in the presence of the Shawnee, shifting from foot to foot, anxious. It is the well-dressed man who takes the lead, addressing the Indian directly.

"I am George Todd," he begins. "Your message to Gideon said that you had found the girl. Is that so, Black Turtle?" The Shawnee regards him impassively. It is not clear whether he has understood.

"Put that in his tongue, Gideon," the well-dressed man says to his companion. "Translate it so that he knows what I am saying."

"I know," Black Turtle says in English. His deep voice has a slight rasp. "We find girl for you."

"Are you sure? She's not dark like the other niggers. She's pale, light-skinned. Younger, too. Her name is Flavia."

The Shawnee nods his head, amused by the intensity of the white man. "Pale girl," he says. "We find her."

"Where?"

Black Turtle says something in his own language, speaking rapidly. He points to the horizon, to their north, and gestures several times as he speaks. The two white men listen carefully, although only Gideon fully understands him.

Gideon rapidly translates for the slim man. "He says that the girl is in a settlement north of here, somewhat east of Cincinnati, near Fort Hamilton, from what I can tell. Black Turtle says the man that she is staying with is known to them. Daniel Flint. In the past, he has come to preach to them about Jesus. Flint has a son, and Black Turtle says there are other men nearby."

"Other men? Can he describe them?"

Again, Gideon and Black Turtle converse; this time, a prolonged, more detailed discussion. Gideon turns back to face Todd when they are finished.

"There are several other men in the settlement. Perhaps one or two runaways, who don't present a threat."

Todd reaches into his jacket for a leather pouch. He produces two Spanish silver dollars from the pouch and hands them across to Black Turtle. The Indian takes them and holds them in his palm. They glint in the late afternoon sun.

"Thank him for his assistance," he says to Gideon, keeping his eyes on the Indian. "Tell him that his skill as a scout has impressed me." Todd pauses, thinking how he will frame his words. "There's more silver for him if he helps in returning the girl to me."

Todd keeps his eyes on Black Turtle. After the translation, the Shawnee nods slightly. He has kept the silver dollars in his free hand. He responds, his deep voice rising and falling.

Gideon listens and then translates for Todd. "He says that it won't be easy. He believes that Flint and his men will fight."

"I will pay him well for his help."

Black Turtle replies rapidly in Shawnee.

"What did he say?" Todd asks.

"He wants to know how you will get the girl back. Whether you will bring more white men."

"It's simple enough. We'll bring enough men that Flint would be a fool to resist. He won't have a choice. The girl's my property. He has no legal right to keep her."

Gideon translates for Black Turtle; there is some back-and-forth between the men.

"He said that they would do it," Gideon says. "I had to promise that you would hold a war council of sorts with him when you arrive at Flint's. And Black Turtle says he will need many silver dollars for all his men. At least three for each warrior."

"Done," Todd says. "As long as he understands that I'm in charge. Council or no council. Is that all he had to say? You two were jabbering for a while."

Gideon hesitates. Todd waves his hand at him in irritation. "What else did he say?"

"Black Turtle wonders why you burn so for the girl. He asks me why you can't find another to take her place? It's just a woman, he says. They are all alike," he pauses, hesitant at finishing the translation, worried that he will give offense, "when they are naked under a man's blanket."

"Tell him it's my business, not his," Todd says. "As long as he and his men get their silver, he should be content. Tell him that. And make sure he understands that I'm in charge."

Gideon and Black Turtle continue to talk. Black Turtle finally nods his assent, his eyes straying to the silver dollars in his palm.

Todd takes that as a signal to speak again. "We will meet you in Cincinnati in one week," he says slowly, occasionally pausing so that Gideon can translate. "Four of us will come from Kentucky. Bring four or five of your men, but keep them outside the town. When you meet us in Cincinnati, you must be alone. We will leave from there to travel to this man Flint's settlement, and get the girl."

Black Turtle doesn't respond. He puts the silver dollars in a deerskin pouch at his side, carefully tying the top flap shut. He then makes his farewell in Shawnee, and slowly returns to the canoe.

After helping to drag the craft back to the river's edge, the other Shawnee climbs into the canoe. Black Turtle pushes the canoe off the bank into the water and then wades out a few feet before jumping in, being careful to keep the canoe balanced. They retrieve their paddles from the floor, and begin paddling. Within a few minutes they have vanished up-river.

Todd and Gideon stand side-by-side and watch the canoe disappear into the dusk.

"You cain't trust them," Gideon says. He shields his eyes from the setting sun. "Been trading with 'em for five years and that's hard-won wisdom." He looks over to the river, at the spot where the canoe was last visible. "I'd not turn my back on that one. He's slippery as a river eel."

Todd appears unmoved. "He knows that I will be in charge. When we see them next, we will have several of my men along, Kentucky men who are good with a rifle and can take care of themselves. Black Turtle won't try anything."

"Why not retrieve the girl without him?"

"He can show us the way to Canaan. He found the girl. None of the slave catchers had any idea where she was."

Gideon isn't satisfied with the answer. "I don't like mixing those greasy red devils into this."

The slim man contemplates the river for a moment, watching the current, the slight chop of the river touching the bank.

"Should anything go wrong, those greasy red devils of yours become quite valuable. They can become the Judas goat. It will be seen as a raid by Shawnee renegades. We'll be back across the river, and any blame will fall on the Indians. Should there be a need, Black Turtle and his men will have their uses, mark my words."

Gideon looks at him, weighing his response. "Ain't supposed to be any trouble, tho'. When Flint sees we've got the numbers, he should give up the girl. Right?"

"That's the idea," Todd says. "But we take the girl, whether Flint likes it or not. It shouldn't concern you overmuch—either way you're getting paid. Let me be the one to worry about the Shawnees, and this man Flint. I know what I'm doing."

TEN

In the morning, Calvin and Judah walked the trail south to Daniel Flint's cabin, which occupied the middle of a clearing along with a small patch of corn. Two trails, leading to the south and west, respectively, began on either side of the clearing. Judah had explained on their walk over that Daniel Flint had been considering building another structure, and at some point opening a general store.

An older man of medium-height with a bushy white beard and piercing blue eyes emerged from the cabin. He strode confidently across the clearing to meet them.

"Welcome to Canaan," he said, extending his hand to Calvin. "I'm Daniel Flint. Any friend of Judah's is a friend of ours."

Calvin shook hands and introduced himself, and Judah quickly explained that they would be traveling east together so that Judah could seek treatment from Dr. Rush in Philadelphia.

"Ye should place your trust in the Lord, not in any doctor," Flint said.

"That may be so for you. I prefer to see a physic. We will leave in short order, before the cold and the snow."

"And Rachel and the child?"

"They will come with us."

Flint grunted dismissively, and turned to Calvin. "Some wouldn't have stood for Judah marrying my Rachel, seeing that he's of the tribe of Abraham. Not Daniel Flint. Just as I believe that we are called to create a

New Jerusalem, I believe it was God's will that my daughter should unite with an Israelite."

"You could come with us to Philadelphia, Daniel," Judah said.

"Why would I do that? My place is here, with the work God has in mind for me. I could not leave those who depend on me." He shook his head, and then addressed Calvin. "Come meet the rest of my family."

They followed Flint as he led the way across the clearing towards the west and proceeded up the trace. One hundred yards up the trail, Flint stopped and waved towards the forest where a small shack was partially hidden in the trees. Flint walked along a muddy pathway to the front of the structure, and knocked on its door. A Negro man dressed in a white shirt and brown trousers emerged from the shack, and then a moment later, a young woman in a simple shift joined him.

"This is Cicero, and his sister, Flavia," Flint said, and Calvin immediately remembered the names from the handbill George Todd was circulating. They had to be the slaves that had escaped from Edgemont Hall.

The girl, Flavia, curtsied, and Calvin noticed her striking looks—an amalgam of African and European features, with smooth tawny skin and curly hair. The handbill had said she was fourteen years of age, but there was nothing childish about her—she had the body of a woman.

"Pleased to meet you, Mr. Tarkington," she said. "Did Mr. Barnabas bring you back from the east?"

"He did, indeed."

She frowned. "But he's not with you?"

"I'm sure he'll be along," Judah said. "I think he and Micah planned to hunt this morning."

"I will be cross with him if he don't come soon," she said. "We've missed him." She had a slight drawl, and the way she spoke reminded Calvin somewhat of Eleanor Todd.

He shook hands with Cicero, briefly glancing at the angry "T" shaped scar on the man's right cheek and then looking away. Cicero grimaced, lifting his hand to touch the scar. Calvin flushed, embarrassed, and saw Flint was watching them.

"Look fully upon Cicero's face, Mr. Tarkington," he said. "Do you mark the brand? Tell him, Cicero, how that happened."

"It was Massa Todd. Las' time I run off, when he ketch me, they brand me. He tell me he send me far away next time."

"Note well the depths of their depravity," Flint said. "Brandin' men like they were animals, beasts of burden. Slaveholders boast of their kindness towards their slaves. But here's the truth, on Cicero's face. He's not unusual. Travel in Kentucky or Virginia, and you will see other Negroes branded by their owners."

Flint was interrupted by the arrival of two men— Barnabas and a much younger man, who proved to be Flint's son, Micah.

"Did you bring me something from your travels?" Flavia asked Barnabas.

"He did," Micah said. He was slight, like his father, with the same intense blue eyes. "Like Barnabas said he would. All the way from New York. Wait 'til ye see it."

"I'm so glad that you're back," Flavia said to Barnabas. "And not just 'cause you brought me something."

Barnabas looked embarrassed. "Let's walk back to the cabin with Micah and Cicero, and I'll check my pack and see what I can find."

He nodded to Calvin and Judah. Flavia skipped up the trail, and Cicero and Micah followed her.

"What did you git her?" Flint asked.

"A comb for her hair," Barnabas answered. "A shawl. And a copy of *The New England Primer*, so she can practice her reading."

Flint frowned. "The shawl and the book are fine gifts," he said. "The comb is vanity."

"She asked for the comb," Barnabas said. "She has so little of her own."

"Very well," Flint said. "Give her the gifts. I will warn her later about the dangers of vanity."

After Barnabas had left, Calvin spoke directly to Flint. "I know that Cicero and Flavia are runaways. Their owner is offering a healthy reward for their return. I saw the handbills in Kentucky on the other side of the river."

"They are children of God," Flint said defiantly. "I helped free them, and I stand before Jehovah with a clear conscience. Just as Shadrach, Meshach, and Abednego refused to obey the laws of Nebuchadnezzar. They knew his laws were not God's laws."

"No magistrate will see it that way," Calvin said. "The law is clear." He understood why many whites helped slaves escape; it was easy to talk of laws and penalties, but another thing to confront frightened humans, desperate for help, and turn away or, worse, betray them to the authorities.

Flint wasn't willing to concede the point. "The Scriptures are clear. 'He hath made of one blood all nations of men for to dwell on all the face of the earth.' On the Day of Judgment, we shall be judged if we have not opposed this evil. The girl has told us of the depravity of her owner, this man George Todd. Constantly after her. Bothering her, like a wild boar in rut. Following the depraved example set by his father, no doubt. When Cicero spoke to Todd about his wicked lust, he threatened to sell Cicero to a plantation in Louisiana. A death sentence. The overseers there work a slave to death in seven or eight years."

"Do you believe that you can shelter them here?" Calvin asked. "Todd is offering a generous bounty for their return."

"What would you have me do? Send them back into bondage?"

"I don't know," Calvin said. "You could offer to buy their freedom."

"And if Todd refuses?"

Calvin hesitated before responding. He didn't have an immediate answer to Flint's question. "You have broken the law. Todd may employ violence to recover what he regards as his property."

Flint's stern expression remained unchanged. "It may take blood to wash away the sin. And if comes to that, I will not flinch." He paused. "Have ye ever seen a coffle, Mr. Tarkington, of Negroes chained together, driven to their next owner? Have ye seen a slave auction? Have ye seen white men force themselves on the young enslaved women? I have seen all of this. I was part of it, and I regret every day that I spent as a driver and trader in Maryland. I will repent for those sins for the rest of me life."

Calvin remained silent. There wasn't anything he could say. There hadn't been a slave auction in New York in years. The Manumission Society had sought boycotts of any merchant who trafficked in slaves, and the importation of Negro slaves into the city had been banned by law.

Flint stared at Calvin. "Do ye think that ye are here by chance, Mr. Tarkington? Ye are here because God wills it so. Where ye will fit in his divine plan, I don't know. But it is not chance that brought ye to Canaan, it's the Divine Hand."

"It was Judah's summons," Calvin said. "Whether that summons was divinely inspired or not, is not for me to say. But I must tell you, Mr. Flint, that I subscribe to the notion of free will. We all make choices which have consequences in the here and now. Your choices will have consequences."

"We will defend ourselves," Flint said. "Aye, we will. 'The stranger that dwelleth with you shall be unto you as one born among you and thou shalt love him as thyself.'"

Calvin had met men like Daniel Flint before—stern, rigid, sure of their rectitude and convinced that they could divine God's Will in a way others could not. Flint had an apt last name—there was a hardness about him, a stone-like obduracy.

"I will bring Rachel and Naomi here to see you before we leave for Philadelphia," Judah said.

"When will that be?" Flint asked.

"Soon. Less than a week."

"May God watch over you, then."

* * *

On their walk back to Judah's cabin, Calvin informed his friend that he had encountered George Todd, Cicero and Flavia's owner, in Maysville and that Barnabas had beaten him badly in a fistfight.

"I didn't fully understand the depths of Barnabas' anger until now," Calvin said. "It seemed out of proportion to the dispute. I had to stop him when Todd was down in the street, defenseless."

"I'm surprised that Barnabas didn't kill him," Judah said. "With the way he feels about Flavia. She has been badly treated by Todd."

"Her escape. Barnabas was involved?"

"We all were," Judah said. "I don't know how much I should tell you about that. Should you ever be called to testify, perhaps it's best you remain ignorant."

"Testify? Hardly. Todd didn't seem like a man who would bother with the courts."

Judah nodded grimly. "From the little Cicero and Flavia have told us about him, I would agree. I fear that he will come here for her, and there will be further violence."

"How did all this come to pass?" Calvin asked.

Judah explained that Flint had met Flavia's brother, Cicero, first. Cicero had run away from Edgemont Hall, and had been helped to escape across the Ohio by a Quaker dealer in horses. He had found his way north to Canaan, where Flint, who was already sheltering two runaway slaves, had taken him in. After living in Canaan for several months, Cicero had pleaded with Flint to help him free his sister.

Flint had prayed over the matter and had opened his King James Bible, at random, and read the first passage he came to, for guidance. He landed on a verse from the book of Isaiah—*I will say to the north, Give up; and to the south, Keep not back: bring my sons from far, and my daughters from the ends of the earth*—and Flint took it as a sign that he was meant to journey to Kentucky and rescue the girl.

There was no arguing with Flint when he believed that he had received a clear and pointed message directly from God; he would not be distracted or dissuaded from pursuing whatever course of action had divine sanction. So Flint and Cicero went back across the river into Kentucky with Flint playing the part of a Virginian looking to buy farmland, and Cicero pretending to be his slave.

"Risky, with that scar," Calvin said. "Especially if they were traveling near Todd's farm."

"Flint believes that his future is in God's hands. He doesn't overly concern himself with risk. Flavia had been watched closely after Cicero escaped. We planned the rescue for a Saturday night. We believed that Flavia's absence would attract less notice on a Sunday, with the Todds at church. It would give us a head start before any serious pursuit could be organized. Cicero got a message to her, and Flavia and another slave, Pompey, arrived at the meeting place. We headed back to Ohio from there."

Judah told him the story of their flight along the Shawnee trace, how George Todd and his men were waiting for them, and how Pompey had been killed. When Todd had discovered that Flavia had left the farm early Sunday morning, he had set out in pursuit with his overseer and hired men. Todd had correctly anticipated their route and had been waiting in ambush. When they heard the first shots, Judah and Barnabas had circled ahead and caught the ambushers by surprise.

"Then you were involved in the death of the man from Edgemont Hall?"

"I was," Judah said. "You must understand that there was little, if any, choice in the matter."

Calvin cursed. If Flint, Barnabas, and Judah were ever arrested and convicted of the killing, they would all hang. There was no judge, or jury, that would accept self-defense as an explanation. Judah had been in the company of thieves, men guilty of stealing slaves. They were the wrongdoers, willing perpetrators of a capital crime.

"I believe it is only a matter of time before Todd learns that Flavia is dwelling here in Canaan," Judah said. "Every time someone new stops by Flint's cabin and catches sight of her, there is risk. She stands out. With a reward for her recovery, we can expect there are slave catchers hunting her."

Calvin had heard of the slave catchers—scouts and woodsmen who put their tracking abilities to work in finding runaway slaves for the bounties offered. The job attracted the most unsavory types, white men who were one step ahead of the law themselves, the shiftless, thieves, and drunks. They would represent a considerable danger if they descended upon Canaan.

"While the law allows Todd to recover his slaves, to do that properly he needs the assistance of a magistrate," Judah said. "The ones in Cincinnati don't care for slavery, and don't particularly want to get mixed up with the runaway question. If he comes for them, he won't bother with the legalities."

"Flint suggested that Todd fancied Flavia."

"No doubt he does. They say that the light-skinned girls have the most trouble. There's nothing to restrain the owner. Flavia's the bastard daughter of an overseer or another white. They will eventually enslave whites if they continue with this pattern. Every time another concubine has another daughter, the child's blood becomes whiter. Flavia's now half African. If she were to carry Todd's child, their progeny would be a quadroon."

"Cicero is her brother, but he's much darker."

"He's her half-brother. A different father, a slave. Flavia has been given better treatment. You hear how well she speaks."

"I understand now why you wish to remove yourself from Canaan," Calvin said. "Flint's fanaticism reminds me of the Jacobins. The same righteousness, the same lack of restraint."

"The truth is that I would want to leave whether or not I had fallen sick," Judah said.

"There's no time to waste. You should see the doctor in Cincinnati before we leave for the east. That will give your wife a few days to prepare for the trip."

"I agree. *Ce n'est pas tout de courir bien, il faut partir a temps.* It's not enough to run well, unless we set out in due time. I'll ask Barnabas to stay and watch over Rachel and Naomi while we are in Cincinnati. He can keep an eye on Flint's place as well."

"Do you think he would be willing to join us on the trip back?" Calvin asked. "If he could come as far as Pittsburgh with us, that would be a help."

"Not with Flavia in Canaan. It was hard enough to persuade him to travel to New York to get you. I don't think he would leave her again."

"He loves her?"

"He does, and she reciprocates."

"It will not be easy for them," Calvin said. "Only a few states allow a white to marry a Negro."

"On the frontier, many don't wait for a preacher before they start living together. No formality. Speaking of which, while you're here you shouldn't dress like an *aristos* with a fine ruffled shirt and elegant waistcoat. Borrow some buckskins from Barnabas for the trip. *À Rome, fais comme les Romains.*"

"We're far from Rome," Calvin said. "And far from any Romans."

"On that, we can agree," Judah said, smiling. "With no fear of contradiction."

ELEVEN

They reached Cincinnati in three days by pushing the pace of their journey, at Judah's insistence. Considering the state of his friend's health, Calvin thought it was a mistake, but he kept his own counsel.

Judah's face was sallow and drawn and, during the trip, he displayed little of the energy Calvin remembered from Paris; when they stopped to eat or rest his fatigue was apparent. He would lie back against a tree trunk and close his eyes—too fatigued to carry on a conversation with Calvin. When they stopped to eat, Judah had little appetite, and Calvin had to urge him to eat his fill of the cornbread and dried meat they carried with them. At times near the end of the day, Calvin worried that Judah might fall off his horse—he appeared to be dozing in the saddle.

"We should rest longer," Calvin suggested at one of their stops.

"No," Judah said, scrambling to his feet. "Not on my account. I have had ample rest."

Calvin welcomed the sight of the cluster of buildings that made up Cincinnati. He was a confirmed city-dweller. While part of him admired the solitude of the wilderness, as he did the vastness of the ocean, he disliked the sense of isolation. Not everyone agreed with him. Some men moved further west when a settler staked out a land claim within ten miles of their cabin.

They went directly to Dr. O'Shea's house. They found him at his kitchen table, finishing his lunch. O'Shea took a swallow of wine from his glass and stood up to greet them.

"Back for an opinion, are you?" he asked. "Payment in advance, if you please. I'll take corn, rye, oats, or Monongahela whiskey if you can't pay cash."

"Pelts?" Judah asked. "Will you take pelts?"

"I will. There's a brisk market for them." He grinned. "You're French. A *ci-devant* aristocrat? Or a Jacobin?"

"Neither. I left that all behind when I came to America."

"A wise man. Best to leave the quarrels of Europe across the Atlantic."

Calvin waited fifteen minutes while O'Shea examined Judah in a nearby room. He overheard snatches of conversation; it was easier to hear Dr. O'Shea's questions than Judah's responses.

When O'Shea completed his examination, he asked Calvin to join them. Calvin could not tell from either O'Shea's countenance, or Judah's, what had transpired.

"Your friend has jaundice," he said to Calvin, and turned to Judah. "It can be seen in the sclera of your eyes—they are tinged yellow—and in the dryness of your skin. Your complaint of excessive weariness, loss of appetite, would match the symptoms of jaundice."

"I could bleed you a cup or two, but you seem weak enough now," O'Shea told Judah. "I have long maintained that purging or bleeding in the face of fatigue can be a mistake. Instead, you should rest and begin a course of medication. I will prepare a draught of soluble tartar in gruel water, which you should take every day now for several weeks. And if you can get raw eggs, you should swallow one a day."

"Will this treatment cure me?" Judah asked.

"It can cure you if your malady has not been caused by your liver," O'Shea said. "I have seen several cases where jaundice was cured."

Judah frowned. "And if it is my liver?"

"We will try other remedies," O'Shea said. "Perhaps then we will bleed, to drain the humors in your body."

"Perhaps?"

O'Shea shrugged. "As I said, I've never been convinced that bleeding was as effective as its proponents claim." He took a piece of paper from his desk and began to write with a quill pen. "We must wait and see how you respond to the treatment regime I have prescribed."

He finished writing and handed the piece of paper to Judah. "It repeats the directions I just gave you. I will give you a month's supply of tartar. You must make the gruel water and dissolve the tartar into it. We must wait and see whether your body can resist the jaundice with the assistance of the tartar."

"Wait and see," Judah repeated skeptically.

"Dr. Rush would tell you the same thing," he said. "There is so much that we do not know. I am not afraid to confess that. My hope is that those involved in the study of natural philosophy, men like Boerhaave and Sydenham, may learn more about the essence of human health. Here it is almost the new century, and we still rely on guesswork and tradition to treat the afflicted. We need more experimentation if we are to make any progress."

There was a knock at the front door. A tall, dark-haired younger man appeared, and O'Shea introduced him as Mr. Williams.

"I'm ready to complete the game," Williams said, glancing over toward the chess board.

"You say that with some relish," O'Shea said. He gave Calvin and Judah a mock face of distress. "It's my misfortune that the only other chess player in Cincinnati never misses an opening."

* * *

Calvin looked forward to a well-cooked meal at Griffin Yeatman's tavern, but Judah shrugged at the thought. When they entered the inn, Calvin noticed that he attracted little interest from the patrons. By wearing buckskins and deerskin moccasins and carrying a long rifle, he no longer stood out the way he had in his New York attire. He had been transformed from merchant-trader to frontiersman, at least on the surface.

They each started with a mug of cider, which Calvin drained twice while Judah was nursing his first drink. Calvin enjoyed the fried venison, broiled chicken, potatoes, cornbread dipped in grease, and apple cobbler; Judah ate some of the venison but could not finish his bowl.

"I'm not hungry," he said. "I need this treatment to restore my appetite."

"That's a shame," Calvin said. "The fare is quite good here."

They were leaving the tavern when a man in buckskins stopped them near the door. "You're friends with Barnabas Hardwick, ain't ye?" The man asked, addressing his question to Judah. He had a ruddy complexion and deep creases in his face, clearly someone who spent most of his life out-of-doors.

"A good friend," Judah said.

"I'm Zeke Pearce. Hunted with Barnabas a time or two. I met a man two days ago who asked if Barnabas had been seen in Cincinnati. Said he wanted to hire him for an expedition. I thought ye might let Barnabas know."

"What's his name?"

"George Todd. From Kentucky, he said. Reputation as a bit of a hothead. Married well, though. Eleanor Randolph, from one of them better Virginia families."

"What was the nature of this expedition? Hunting? Surveying?"

"He didn't quite say," Pearce said. "He brought Gideon Carvey, the trader, with him and a Shawnee, Black Turtle. Not the most savory, neither of 'em. Black Turtle's known for stealin' horses, though it ain't been proven by anyone. I'd not show my back to him in the woods."

"No others? Just those three?" Judah asked.

"That I know of. Black Turtle always has a few braves with him. They maybe stayed out of town."

"Did they ask after anyone else?"

Pearce shook his head, and then hesitated. "Wait, that ain't so. Todd asked about Daniel Flint. Wondered if any of us had been by his place and seen a young slave girl, a runaway, there. Light-skinned, a pretty piece. Not a one had."

"Is he still in town?"

"Not that I know. This was two days ago. Cain't say any of us were sorry to see 'em leave. Damned slave catchers should stay on their side of the river."

Judah thanked the man, and the moment they were on the street, he pulled Calvin aside, gripping him by the left elbow.

"We must leave for Canaan at once," he said. "If George Todd is asking about Daniel Flint and Flavia, he may be headed there."

"What is Todd doing with Black Turtle?" Calvin asked. "That's strange."

"Not if you're hunting for runaways. Black Turtle knows the lay of the land as well as any man."

"Why was Todd asking about Barnabas? Looking to hire him?"

"I don't know," Judah said. "God forbid that Todd and his men encounter Daniel Flint in Canaan."

"Barnabas is keeping watch," Calvin said. "I agree we should return promptly. We should wait until the morning. We'll make much better time if we're rested."

Judah nodded. "At dawn, then."

TWELVE

New York

After Devlin Phelan's unwelcome and troubling visit to Greenwich Street, Katharine did not wait to take action—she felt that she could not risk living alone in the house, not with Calvin away. That afternoon she ventured to Water Street and asked Jean Laurent for his assistance in arranging for servants.

"Calvin wanted me to hire a new housekeeper," she explained to the slightly-built Frenchman. "I resisted the idea, but now I believe that he was correct. I'd like to find a couple, if I could, so there would be a manservant who could help with the more taxing work, such as cutting firewood and fetching water from our well. Perhaps someone who has worked for Tarkington & Scott in the past?"

Laurent thought for a moment and then, to Katharine's great relief, nodded. "I believe there may be a couple who would be interested. Your husband knows Mr. Hopkins from the voyage to China in '94. He was one of the crew. A solid, dependable man. He fell last year and hurt his leg, so he hasn't been back to sea."

A day later, Arnold and Tabitha Hopkins arrived at Greenwich Street for a brief interview. Katharine immediately liked Tabitha, a stout, matronly woman. Arnold Hopkins proved to be a red-faced, brawny middle-aged man who walked with a slight limp. She agreed to their employment, and asked them to return the next day to begin their duties.

Once the Hopkins returned to Greenwich Street the following day, Katharine waited until Tabitha was occupied in the kitchen before approaching her husband. "Mr. Hopkins, I have a request to make."

"Yes, ma'am?"

"At times, there may be strangers or others who call at the house. With my husband traveling, I would be more comfortable knowing that you are nearby in the event that I require your assistance."

"My assistance?" He squinted at her, not understanding.

"Sadly, these days there are some men who may believe they have license to say or do things they would never do if my husband were at home. While I doubt it will be necessary, I might ask you to act as my guardian, of sorts."

"Be glad to, ma'am," he replied. "Arnold Hopkins won't stand for unseemly behavior, you can rest assured."

"Thank you, Mr. Hopkins. That's a relief."

* * *

She had been delighted when Livingston Rhodes stopped by Greenwich Street a few days later. He was dressed in a shabby gray coat and worn blue shirt, and one of his stockings needed darning. She wondered if Livingston was short of money, although he didn't seem depressed or anxious.

"How are you faring?" he asked her. "Are you sleeping well? How is your appetite?"

"I'm fine," she told him. "Please don't worry about me. I'm not the first woman to carry a child, Livingston, and I'll manage just fine."

"Glad to see that you have help in the house."

"Calvin was right about that," she said. "He wanted me to hire a housekeeper, and I had resisted. It's a comfort to have Mr. and Mrs. Hopkins here with me."

"I know Hopkins from the voyage to Canton. He's a good man. Dependable."

"And Calvin knows him, so he won't come home to find a complete stranger."

"I've brought news from Ireland," Livingston said, pulling out a folded newssheet from his coat pocket. "It's the talk of the town. There's more news of the rising. Defeats for the rebels at Knightstown Bog and Ballyboughal. More atrocities, as no quarter was given by the British."

"What of Mr. Tone? And the French?"

Livingston looked at her sadly. "No word. They haven't budged. It's too late in the game, I would think." He tugged at his chin, considering something. "That man we met on Bowling Green. Phelan. Why is he here in New York and not in Ireland? Or with Tone in France?"

"I don't know. Sean thought he was more committed to the cause of Devlin Phelan than to that of a free Ireland."

Livingston grinned. "Revolutions attract more scoundrels than saints. I didn't care for the man, if the truth be told."

"I don't either," she said. "It would suit me if he went to Ireland and never came back."

* * *

She had hoped against hope that she had seen the last of Devlin Phelan, but when he knocked on the front door a week later, she at least felt better prepared. She reluctantly invited him into the foyer, confident that with Arnold Hopkins in the house that she had only to call for him if Phelan overstepped the bounds. She decided to take a firm stand at the start.

"I thought I made my position clear," she said. "You're not welcome here. Our manservant waits in the kitchen, and if you should make any further assaults on my person, I shall immediately call him. He's a large man, a Jack Tarr, and he's deeply loyal to the family."

"You've heard the latest news from Ireland?" he asked. "The sad news."

"I have."

"You supported the cause, once. A free, independent Ireland."

"I still do. I have other responsibilities, now. To my husband."

"Your husband. I've been asking around, Kate. It's not often that a rich New York merchant marries his housekeeper, even if she's a fine-looking woman. It came as a surprise to most around here. And you're Irish, and you know how proper society feels about us. We're drunken Paddies and secret Jesuits, even those of us that are Protestant."

"What does that matter?"

"I will ask again. What's your reputation worth to you?"

"I don't worry about my reputation," she said. "I've done nothing to be ashamed of."

"I believe that your high-and-mighty husband doesn't know about your past," he said. "I think that it slipped your mind, Kate, during the wooing. You're a clever woman. You thought it was better to leave certain things unsaid. Bury the past. What with Sean being gone, who would be none the wiser?"

She remained silent.

"With what I have learned, I'm here to make you an offer. I'll keep my mouth shut about your past for a price." He looked at her. "One hundred silver dollars. That's fair. Or I can start telling stories. I don't think that you want me to do that."

"You must be mad."

"The money wouldn't be for me, it would be for the Irish cause, of course, in a way." He looked over her shoulder into the drawing room. "I know that specie can be difficult to find on short notice. I'll bet there's quite a bit of fine silver in the house you could sell. Or your jewelry. If your husband noticed, you could claim that you got carried away by the love of the cause. He might be angry, but I think it'd be better to confess that than to admit that you were Sean Daly's whore."

"You're despicable."

"Am I? Most would say lying to your husband is despicable."

"I haven't lied, not that it's any of your business."

"If you can't raise all the money, there are other ways you can pay," he said.

"Leave now," she said.

"I'll go. Think about how ye'd like to pay. I'll give ye three days, and then I'll be back. I'm not a greedy man. If you're short on the dollars, I only expect to be welcomed in your bed for a nice roll. I promise you'll have no complaints."

"When Hell freezes over," she said.

He smirked and left.

She detested the man. She hated the way he looked at her, staring openly at her breasts, and then boldly bringing his eyes to meet hers. She knew full well how to spurn the unwanted advances of men—she had been doing so since she was twelve years old—but there was something particularly repulsive about his behavior. It was so brazen.

He would never have dared to take such liberties if Calvin had been there. She thought of her husband as a gentle man, but she had once or twice sensed his underlying toughness. She knew him well enough that he would have dealt swiftly, and forcefully, with any man bothering her.

* * *

Katharine didn't sleep well the next two nights, trying to decide what to do. If only Calvin were there—she could have told him the truth, and then her husband could have decided how to handle Devlin Phelan. She had no doubt that if she had the chance to explain things to Calvin, he would tell Phelan to go to the devil.

But Calvin wasn't there with her. If she rejected Phelan's demand for money, and he reacted by blackening her name, how would Calvin react when he returned? She doubted any of his well-bred friends would rise to her defense. Irish newcomers weren't popular in New York, and too many of the thieves, pickpockets, and whores in the city had come from Dublin or Cork or Limerick.

She had never said anything to Calvin, but she had heard that Mayor Varick detested the Irish. According to Francis O'Connor, Varick had sided with an arrogant alderman named Furman in a dispute with two Irish ferrymen. Furman had beaten the men with a cane, claiming they were insolent, and had them arrested for insulting a city official. There had been a grossly one-sided trial in mayoral court, the ferrymen had been convicted, and Varick had sentenced them to jail. His behavior had been bitterly resented by the Irish in the city.

"For some of the Dutch, we're no better than the blacks," O'Connor had warned her. "They don't want us here, Kate, and the English aren't much better."

She had other reasons for concern. She had been relying on the generosity of her relatives before she met Calvin, and she dreaded even the thought of returning to a life on the edge of poverty, however remote that prospect might be. She had believed that she had left that behind when she married a man of wealth and influence. Katharine loved the Greenwich Street residence, its long drawing room, spacious kitchen, numerous fireplaces, and comfortable bedrooms.

She didn't want to jeopardize her new life. Wouldn't it be better if she gave Phelan some money? She could make it clear that it was a one-time payment—never to be repeated. Perhaps Phelan would be satisfied enough to leave her alone. It was worth a try, she told herself. If she gave him an outright refusal, he might very well follow through on his threats and spread malicious stories about her.

She didn't make her mind up until the morning of the third day. She went to the ornately carved wooden chest in Calvin's study, unlocked it, and took fifty Spanish silver dollars. She placed them in a leather sack with a drawstring.

Devlin Phelan did not appear until late in the afternoon. When he knocked on the door, Katharine had Tabitha answer it. She made Phelan wait in the drawing room for ten minutes before she saw him.

She remained standing and kept her distance when she addressed him. "I have given this some thought. I will not pay blackmail. Not a penny. My husband knows the truth." She paused. "You once believed in an independent and free Ireland and you made sacrifices for that, just as Sean and the others did. So I'm willing to help you now, with some conditions. You must never return here. This is the last time we will have any association."

"I see. And what form will this help take?"

She placed the leather sack on the nearest table. "There is fifty Spanish in that bag. That should put you back on your feet."

"Ah, you should have been a Jesuit, Kate. You won't pay blackmail, will ye? But silver in a bag. I'll take this as a down payment on the one hundred that you owe me."

"No, not a down payment. This is all I will ever pay you."

Phelan grinned. "Sure of yourself, aren't you? You could always take me into one of the fine bedrooms here and work off the difference."

"I find you disgusting," she said. "There are plenty of women in New York you can take to bed with the money I've given you. The money that's supposed to go to the cause."

"That may well be," he said. "But I fancy you, Kate."

"You have the money. Take it and leave. Should you return, I'll have our manservant turn you out."

"We shall see about that," Phelan said. "You're in my debt, Kate, and I'll get paid my full measure, one way or the other."

"I loathe you," she said. "You're a bastard. Do you hear me?"

He shook the sack of dollars so that the silver jingled. "That's what I'm hearing," he said. "The sound of silver. I'll take your leave now, but I'll be back. You can count on that."

PART FOUR

THIRTEEN

The Northwest Territory

The first glimmer of dawn brings light to the clearing. The few remaining rows of unharvested corn cast long shadows on the ground.

It promises to be a mild day, with warmer temperatures than could be expected for November in a latitude this far north. There is not much of a breeze, and the trees in the forest are still, undisturbed by even the slightest wind.

Above, a small flock of birds—brown-and-buff colored woodcocks—glide silently south, not fooled by the weak sun, their migration for the winter already underway.

Ten men wait on the outskirts of the clearing, hidden from view in the trees and scrub underbrush of the forest. There are four white men and six Shawnee of the Piqua clan. While they are allies for the moment, the two groups keep a distinct, and wary, distance from each other. All of the men are heavily armed, and the faces of the Indians have been painted—streaks of dark red and black—in preparation for battle.

Off to one side, two of the whites and a Shawnee meet and talk quietly. As they converse, they steal glances at a ramshackle cabin at the far end of the clearing. The taller of the whites keeps shaking his head angrily at something the Shawnee is saying.

They keep looking over at the cabin where a slight plume of smoke rises from its makeshift chimney. Its simple front porch is made of wood planking. A solitary chair, stationed at the far end, has the look of an afterthought.

The men remain in waiting; most remain hidden behind the nearest trees. They watch the cabin intently.

Finally, the taller white man and his Shawnee counterpart reach agreement. They return to their respective groups, and both begin to give orders.

At a whispered command from his leader, one Shawnee drops to the ground and begins to crawl forward towards the cabin. Within a few moments, he has moved close to the porch and then another Indian follows him. They position themselves on either side of the cabin.

Ten minutes pass. The Shawnee wait stoically; the whites fidget and shift impatiently. The door to the cabin opens and a boy of perhaps sixteen or seventeen comes out and walks into the clearing carrying a pail. The two Shawnee wait until he is fifty feet from the cabin and then step in front of the porch, closing off any escape back to the cabin.

The tall Shawnee steps from the tree so the boy can see him. The boy cries out, dropping the pail, frightened at the sight of the Indian's garishly painted face. He looks back towards the cabin and sees the other Indians and realizes that he is trapped.

The leader of the whites approaches the boy. He says something in a low voice and the boy shakes his head. The white man repeats himself, insistent, but the boy will not agree. The other white man, who earlier had been translating, steps forward and holds the boy by the right arm.

The leader does not hesitate. He moves into the clearing, and takes a position fifteen yards from the cabin's front door. He looks around to make sure the men are stationed where he wants them.

"Flint," the man calls out loudly. "Daniel Flint. Show yourself. This is George Todd. We have your boy. All we want is what is ours."

There is no response at first, but then the sound of movement within the cabin. The door swings open and a white-haired man steps out. His unclubbed hair flows down his back, and he is dressed in a linsey-woolsey shirt and breeches. He looks around the clearing at the men congregated there, taking in the presence of the Indians.

"What's the meaning of this?" he asks.

Todd steps closer to the porch. "You know why we are here," he says in a conversational tone. He is so matter-of-fact that he could be asking for the loan of tools or for directions. "We're here for Flavia."

"What sort of man bargains with a boy's life?"

Todd lowers his voice. "What sort of a man steals? What sort of a man breaks the commandment not to covet his neighbor's goods? Bring Flavia to me, and we won't harm you or your boy. Despite what happened back in Kentucky with the man you killed, Lawton Chance. I don't want any more blood shed. Just what is mine."

"What is yours?" Flint shakes his head. "Ye cannot own another human. It's an abomination. The Lord Almighty will look after Micah. I'll not trade Flavia for him. Abraham was asked to sacrifice his son Isaac on Mount Horeb, and he obeyed, and I can do no less."

"You're wrong, old man," Todd says. He speaks in a tone that only Flint can hear. "The girl isn't worth your life or your boy's. She's no innocent. Half of my niggers would be rutting with her if I turned my back. She isn't worth it. You can't stop us so you might as well turn her over to me. She's mine by law."

"She's not yours," Flint says. "Not in the eyes of God."

"Stubborn old fool. What can you do? Nothing, and we both know it. Give us the girl."

The largest of the Shawnees, Black Turtle, is watching the conversation between Todd and Flint. When he sees the unyielding look on Flint's face, he raises the tomahawk in his left hand, a signal to his men.

Flint shakes his head and starts to retrace his steps to the cabin, turning his back and showing no fear of the men behind him. For a moment, both the Shawnee and the whites are frozen in place by the old man's boldness.

Flint is no more than five yards from the cabin when Black Turtle motions to his men. Two fire their rifles at the same time and Flint staggers as he is hit in the shoulder and lower back. He falls heavily to the ground.

To their amazement, he rises to his feet, and stumbles forward, determined to reach the cabin. This time, Black Turtle raises his own rifle, and he pulls the trigger as Flint starts up the porch. The flintlock discharges loudly, and Flint staggers again and then falls to the porch floor, a dead weight. This time he does not rise; he lies there, unmoving.

From either side of the cabin, Shawnee appear and drag Flint's body, face down, into the clearing, leaving a trail of blood on the ground.

Todd turns to Micah. "Where is she, boy? Don't make your father's mistake."

Micah silently raises his hand and points up the trail. "She's there," he whispers. "A shack. A few hundred yards."

Todd makes his way up the trail until he reaches the hut. "Flavia!" he calls out. "I know that you are in there. Come out now and we won't hurt the boy."

There are sounds of movement inside the shack and the door slowly opens. Flavia steps out onto the porch, hesitating, unsure of what awaits.

There is another sudden burst of movement. Micah has pulled free and now rushes at Todd, a knife in his hand. There is a shot from the rifle of Gideon, the interpreter, and the boy drops the knife and clutches at his side, an astonished look on his face. He sinks to his knees, bewildered by what has happened.

"What?" he asks. "What did you do?"

Then Micah drops to the ground and curls up, almost as if he is ready to sleep. One of his legs begins to move spasmodically, thrashing about, and then it stops, and finally the boy is completely still.

Flavia has not left the porch. She stands there, frozen by the sudden violence that has unfolded before her. Todd approaches the porch, his hand extended.

"Come here," he says, his voice low and gentle. "Time to come home."

She leaves the porch and moves slowly across the clearing until she is standing in front of him. She looks down, not making eye contact.

"That's my girl," Todd says. He places his hand on her shoulder, possessively. She flinches slightly, but remains still.

Todd motions to one of the white men. "Take her to the horses," he says. "I'll be there shortly."

Not twenty feet away, one of the Shawnees has Flint's white hair gathered in his hand, holding the dead man's head up. He proceeds to tomahawk the hair and some of the scalp free from Flint's head. Gideon turns away in revulsion.

"They shouldn't be scalpin' 'em," he says to Todd.

"What does it matter? Flint and his boy are dead anyway."

"It ain't right what Black Turtle and them are doing."

Todd shrugs. "Perhaps not. However, we're not in a position to object too strenuously. We have what we came for. That's enough."

Black Turtle, the Shawnee leader, approaches them and speaks with Gideon.

"He wants his silver," Gideon says. "He wants it now."

"He and his men must put the bodies in the cabin and then burn it," Todd says. "Then they will get paid."

Gideon explains to Black Turtle, who grunts and instructs his men. Within minutes they have dragged Flint and Micah into the cabin and set it afire. Smoke rises into the air and flames consume the dry wood of the porch and then spread to the roof.

"Let's get to the horses," Todd says to Gideon. "Quick, now. Pay Black Turtle. It's in our interests to put some distance between us and this place."

The trader grimaces and turns away, the bag of silver dollars in his hand. "Far as I'm concerned, cain't get out of this damn place fast enough."

FOURTEEN

After learning of George Todd's sudden presence in the Northwest Territory, Judah had insisted that they push the pace on their return trip to Canaan. It fell to Calvin to remind Judah that their horses needed rest, and that blundering about after dark was courting disaster. It was better to rise at first light and return to the trail when they could see clearly. Judah reluctantly agreed.

Calvin understood his friend's desire to reach home as soon as humanly possible. Judah feared that Todd might attack Canaan suddenly and without warning, and he worried for the safety of all there, particularly his wife and child. Calvin tried reassuring him that all would be well under Barnabas' watchful eye.

"He's one man," Judah said sourly. "Barnabas can't be everywhere. We should never have left for Cincinnati."

"Recriminations serve no purpose," Calvin replied. "We can't be sure what Todd is planning to do. Barnabas and Daniel Flint know the danger. I'm sure Barnabas is scouting nearby."

"I fear that it was a grievous mistake to leave the two of them alone to defend Canaan."

"Perhaps. We can do nothing to alter that fact now. We must accept what Fate has in store for them and for us."

"Must you be such a Stoic, Calvin?"

"Epictetus taught that happiness lies in ceasing to worry about those things which are beyond the power of our will. I try my best to follow that advice, to master my emotions."

"That's not for me," Judah said. "I cannot experience life at such a remove. It's too cold a philosophy for my taste."

"I will not pretend that it's easy. After Sarah's death, it was in the writings of Epictetus and Marcus Aurelius and a Fleming, Justus Lipsius, that I found whatever solace I could. They understood what it was to suffer a loss, and how one had to carry on as best as one could. Today I worry, of course, but I have learned not to torment myself with bitterness and regrets."

Calvin did not voice one of his continuing worries—Judah's health. The treatment that Dr. O'Shea had prescribed had done little to improve his friend's appetite, and it had not altered the yellowish tinge to his skin. Twice Judah had stopped to retch by the side of the trail, and Calvin was dismayed to see he left blood behind on the leaves.

They rode directly to Flint's property, and they found a chilling scene awaiting them. Flint's cabin had been burned to the ground, and all that remained were ashes, charred timbers, and an ugly scar in the clearing. Judah surveyed the devastation, his jaw set grimly, and turned to Calvin. "It's what I feared."

Before Calvin could reply, he heard his name being called. A moment later, Barnabas appeared at the entry point of the far trail. He cradled his long rifle in his arms, and Calvin noticed that he had a tomahawk belted to his waist.

"They attacked two days ago," he told them. "They killed Flint and Micah, and took Flavia. I found signs of Shawnee. Boot prints left by whites, too."

"We learned in Cincinnati that George Todd had been seen in the company of Black Turtle," Judah said. "It must have been them. Tell me of my family." Judah kept his face composed, but Calvin knew that he had to be in agony wondering about the fate of his wife and daughter.

"Rachel and Naomi are safe. I left Cicero to guard them at your cabin. I've been checking the trails, looking for you."

"How is it that Cicero wasn't killed or taken?"

"He wasn't here. He stayed at my place that night, so we could hunt in the morning. We left at dawn, and were a few miles south of Flint's place.

We didn't know there was trouble until we saw the smoke when they fired the cabin. They were gone when we got here. From what I could tell from the tracks they left, it was ten or so men, with horses. They split up about a mile from the cabin, with the Shawnee heading west, and the others south. I figured it was Todd, and I thought about following him and trying to free Flavia, but I didn't like the odds."

"You made the right choice," Judah said. "Todd and his men would have been ready for you."

"I will bring Flavia back," Barnabas said. "Now that you're here, I reckon I can start."

"By yourself?" Calvin asked. "That seems foolhardy."

"Cicero will come with me. We'll travel light. We'll get help from Cicero's friends in Kentucky, like the last time. It worked once, and I don't see why it won't work again."

"I will go with you," Judah said.

Calvin shook his head. "I must counsel against this course of action. Todd will be waiting for you, Barnabas. If you're intent on a rescue, why not wait until the spring, when Todd will have let his guard down?"

"And leave Flavia with that brute? Never." Barnabas glared at him.

"What of justice for Daniel and Micah?" Judah asked. "Killed in cold blood. Surely they deserve justice."

"We should approach the magistrate in Cincinnati," Calvin said. "George Todd is the suspect in two murders. He should be brought to account."

"Will the magistrate act?" Judah asked.

"We must convince him to act. We should see what we can do with the law on our side."

"The law will not be on my side when it comes to getting Flavia back," Barnabas said. "I pay that little heed. I'll free her, law or no law."

* * *

They left for Cincinnati the following morning. Judah and Rachel packed up their few possessions, aware that they would not be returning to Canaan. Judah, Rachel, and Naomi rode on one horse, Calvin and Cicero on another, and Barnabas on a third. It was a slow, grim journey, made miserable by the cold, relentless drizzle that began to fall on the second day, soaking them to the bone.

Calvin was alarmed by Judah's failing health. He continued to eat little, and there was no improvement in his color. When they reached Cincinnati, and had settled Rachel and Naomi in Mrs. Bainbridge's boarding house, Calvin accompanied Judah to Dr. O'Shea. The Irishman answered Judah's knock on his front door.

"Back so soon?" he asked, a frown on his face.

"I've not gotten better," Judah said. "The treatment has not worked."

"Come in, then."

O'Shea took Judah into a side room to examine him. When they returned, Judah could not disguise his exhaustion. O'Shea suggested that he lie down on a couch, and within minutes Judah started to nod off. Within moments he was sleeping soundly. O'Shea looked over at him with interest.

"The human organism fascinates me," he said to Calvin. "It seeks to conserve strength when under assault. Let us hope that sleep acts as a defense and restorative for your friend."

O'Shea went to the cupboard and found a bottle. He poured two cups of whiskey and handed one to Calvin.

"Your health," he said, raising the cup.

"Your health," Calvin replied.

O'Shea tossed down his whiskey, smacking his lips before speaking. "It appears your friend's jaundice has been caused by some other morbidity, perhaps a disease associated with his internal organs. I will bleed him when he awakes, at his insistence. He says he has a trip he must take, but that would be very unwise. In fact, he should stay here under my care for the next few days."

"He will not want to do that."

"That may be so. But his health is precarious. If he travels now, in this cold, he may worsen rapidly."

"He will want to go, nonetheless. A matter of honor."

"Ah, the honor of the French. One of their weaknesses. Just as the whiskey we're enjoying is the bane of the Irish. That and our attraction to hopeless causes."

"My wife is from Dublin," Calvin said. "I hope that I'm not completely a hopeless cause."

O'Shea laughed. "You appear to be a man of many parts, Mr. Tarkington. A fish out of water in a place like this."

"It's true I'm more at home on the deck of a brig than on the back of a horse, but I'm adapting to the Northwest Country."

"As must we all." O'Shea poured himself another cup of whiskey. "You must prevail upon Mr. Gomez that he must rest. It would be folly for him to attempt anything strenuous. He shrugged. "Of course, I can only prescribe, not command. You are his friend, and I would hope he'd listen to you."

* * *

Calvin helped a weak and drawn Judah to Mrs. Bainbridge's after Dr. O'Shea had bled him. Then he and Barnabas went to the courthouse near the center of Cincinnati and found the magistrate, a Pennsylvanian named David Chester Tennant.

Tennant was a soft-spoken, formal man in his mid-forties with a deep bass voice who greeted them quietly, and invited them to sit down in two sturdy dark wooden chairs. Calvin noticed a handsome hall clock in the corner; according to the clock's face, it was from the shop of Simon Willard, a well-known Boston clockmaker.

They had decided before arriving that Calvin would take the lead in presenting the situation to the authorities. He got straight to the point.

"We are here about two murders," he began. "Daniel Flint and his son Micah, killed in Canaan, a settlement north of Fort Hamilton some four days ago. We seek a warrant against the murderer and his accomplices."

"And who might you be?" Tennant asked. He was polite but wary.

"Calvin Tarkington. A merchant from New York. My firm is Tarkington & Scott."

"Tarkington? Are you any relation to Alexander Tarkington?" There was a noticeable softening of Tennant's tone.

"My older brother."

"Met him once," Tennant said. "During the war, at Brandywine. Cut quite a figure. On General Washington's staff, wasn't he?"

"He was," Calvin said. "Did you serve in the Continental Army, then, sir?"

"I did, under General Greene. Is your brother active in the firm?"

"Alexander passed on six years ago."

"My condolences." Having established a connection with Calvin, Tennant appeared to lose some of his wariness. Calvin had always marveled at the bond between the officers of the Continental Army, most of whom were members of the Society of the Cincinnati. He had benefited from his brother's inclusion in that elite group, for there had been several times in the past when members of the order, both American and French, had assisted Calvin.

"Now, what is this about murder?" Tennant asked.

"Daniel Flint and his son Micah were shot and scalped by Shawnee at the direction of a Kentucky man, George Todd."

Tennant frowned. "A nasty business. What was the cause for these murders? The motive?"

This, Calvin knew, would prove to be the hard part of the conversation. He had to tell the story of the killings, and explain about Flavia and her presence in Canaan. Since he did not know where Tennant stood on the question of slavery, he had to be careful in what he said.

"The dispute between Flint and his attackers began over a mulatto girl named Flavia," he said.

"A mulatto? Free or a slave?"

"That was at the heart of the dispute. Daniel Flint maintained that she was free now that she was living in the Northwest Territory. Todd did not. Rather than producing her documents and involving the law, he came to Canaan with the idea of taking her back with him forcibly."

"Taking her back? She ran away?"

"Flint's hands were not clean in this matter. He had harbored her. Todd has been looking for Flavia for months. He posted a bounty. He must have learned that she was in Canaan, and hired the Shawnees to help him in regaining her."

Tennant considered what Calvin had said, scratching under his wig, delaying his response. "This is a serious allegation that you make, Mr. Tarkington. Capital crimes. Are you certain of the facts?"

"I'm certain," Calvin said.

"There are witnesses? Men who saw the attack, and who will swear that Mr. Todd directed it?"

"Mr. Hardwick came upon the bodies of Flint and his son," Calvin said, nodding to Barnabas. "They had fired Flint's cabin."

"And who might you be?" Tennant asked, turning to Barnabas.

"Barnabas Hardwick. A fur trader and hunter for the Army. Fort Washington and Fort Hamilton."

"Your claim, then, is that it was a group of men, both Indians and whites, who attacked?

Barnabas nodded.

"If you did not witness the attack, how can you assert that?"

"They left a trail. Footprints. Tracks from their horses. The Shawnee split off after a while."

"What about the girl?" Calvin asked. "Doesn't Todd's possession of her prove that he was in Canaan?"

Tennant shook his head. "Can you prove how she was returned to his custody?"

"It was Todd," Barnabas said grimly. "Zeke Pearce can testify that Todd was in Cincinnati asking about the girl a week before the attack."

"Suggestive, but not determinative," Tennant said. He cleared his throat. "I have no reason to doubt your account, Mr. Hardwick, but I cannot proceed with a bench warrant based on the facts before me. By your own admission, there are no witnesses to the attack. No one who saw this man Todd at the scene. Could it not be renegade Indians? They might have taken this girl."

"Todd is the logical suspect," Calvin said.

"Logical or not, I can only proceed on the basis of sound evidence." Tennant sighed. "I wish I could help, but there are limits to what I can do."

"We're sure it was Todd."

"That may very well be the truth. But I must caution you against seeking private justice, Mr. Tarkington." Tennant rose to his feet. "There is no room for such lawlessness in this Territory."

"On the contrary," Calvin replied bitterly. "It appears there is plenty of room."

* * *

Calvin and Barnabas returned to the boarding house, where they found Judah resting on a divan in the common room. Calvin quickly told them about their failure with David Chester Tennant.

"No surprise," Judah said. "Remember, I was a lawyer in Paris. This magistrate is correct to be cautious about proceeding. Without witnesses or other evidence, there is only a circumstantial case to be made against Todd."

"It was worth the try," Calvin replied.

"*Mais oui bien sûr.* Our path becomes apparent. We must leave for Kentucky as soon as I have my strength back. A few days, at most."

"You don't need to come," Barnabas said. "Cicero knows the lay of the land. Once we have Flavia, and we're back in the woods, we'll be fine. I know I can shake Todd if he follows."

"You need more rifles, in the event that something goes wrong. I must insist that you wait a few days so that I may go."

"If it's a question of another rifle, I can take your place," Calvin said. "In truth, I believe that I'm a better shot." He looked over at Barnabas. "But Barnabas must agree that our goal will be solely to free Flavia. It's not to exact revenge on Todd. I won't join in that."

"This ain't your fight," Barnabas said. "Why should I agree to any conditions?"

"If it's Judah's fight, then it's mine. My conditions are practical in nature. If you free Flavia, but kill Todd in the doing, you become a fugitive with a capital crime hanging over your head. Recover Flavia without violence, and you can return east with us, beyond Todd's reach."

"I've not agreed to this substitution," Judah said. "Let us wait until tomorrow before we decide. I should be on the road to recovery by then."

* * *

In the morning, however, Judah was too weak to get out of bed. Rachel asked Calvin to fetch Dr. O'Shea, and after a brief examination of Judah, O'Shea joined them in the parlor.

"I advise against any more bleeding," he told them. "He is too weak."

"What do you advise?" Rachel asked.

"Rest. Encourage him to eat. I will return tomorrow to see how he's faring."

"Travel is out of the question, then?" Calvin asked.

O'Shea arched his eyebrows. "Travel would be most unwise."

Calvin found Barnabas at Yeatman's Tavern and shared the news about Judah's worsened condition.

"I can't wait," Barnabas said. "I can't abide the thought of her at his mercy."

"Then I must take Judah's place. He is in no condition to object."

Barnabas glanced around the tavern. "We need one more. I've decided to approach Zeke Pearce about coming with us. No better hunter in the Territory. He's to meet me here."

They sat and drank ale while they waited for Pearce. When Pearce arrived, he came over to their table.

"We've had a great run of luck," he began. "Huntin' black bear. We've shot sixteen, caught 'em before they went into hibernation. A few still out there, Barnabas, if ye have a hankerin' to hunt. The skins have been fetchin' a goodly price. Five dollars a skin. But what's more, the tanners are payin' a dollar a gallon for bear oil. Imagine that, a dollar. A man could get rich. We're averagin' fifteen gallons a carcass."

Barnabas cleared his throat. "Unfortunately, I'm not here about hunting. There's sad news to relate, Zeke. Disturbing news. Daniel Flint is dead. Killed by the orders of that Kentucky man, George Todd, you met here in Cincinnati. The one with Black Turtle."

Pearce grimaced. "What of Flint's boy, Micah?"

"Killed as well. Judging from the bodies, both of them were scalped."

"Scalped," Pearce repeated. "How can this be?"

"Looks like Todd brought a war party with him, turned Black Turtle and his men loose on Flint. They were there to snatch freed slaves."

"What is it that you propose?" Pearce was all business—he could have been inquiring after an expedition to hunt for bear or to set traps.

"We propose to travel to Kentucky and free the slave he took, a young girl named Flavia."

Pearce showed his teeth in what passed for a smile. "If she's a slave, she's somebody's property. Sounds like Todd ain't gonna agree to let her go. A girl, ye say. I'll bet he didn't come all the way from Montgomery County because he liked her cooking."

"His attachment is an improper one," Calvin said.

Pearce spat on the floor. "I'd say so. Mixin' the colors is wrong, whether a woman is slave or free. Black ain't meant to lie with white, nor red with white. Ask me, they never should brung them darkies here."

"You don't care for Negroes?" Calvin asked, surprised.

"Not a nigger-hater, nor a nigger-lover. Don't git me wrong. But this country should be for white men, free men. Daniel Flint had it all mixed up. The children of Ham ain't meant to dwell with the children of Shem."

"Will you help us recover the girl?" Barnabas asked.

"Could care less if some nigger girl stays a slave. I'll go 'cause ye stood by me afore, and no white man should use Shawnee 'gainst other whites. I'll stand with ye. When ye plannin' to leave for Kentucky?"

"We were waiting on your answer. If you're coming, we'll leave tomorrow."

"Ye been huntin' with me, Barnabas," Pearce said. "Ye know I take orders from no man."

"I know that."

"Yer friend understan'?" Pearce glanced over at Calvin.

"You're welcome to accompany us," Calvin said. "With this one condition. We seek only to free the girl. This is not a private mission of vengeance or revenge."

Pearce looked at Barnabas. "Ye agreed to this?"

"I did."

"Alrighty, then. If Todd don't object when we steal his slave, we leave him be. Course, I reckon the Quakes would say we ain't stealin' 'cause the girl wasn't rightly owned in the first place."

* * *

Calvin employed Jack O'Shea's desk to write the necessary letters in the event things went badly on their mission to Kentucky. He had sailed enough for Tarkington & Scott to have embraced the mariner's fatalism about the future. It was not the first time Calvin had left instructions on what needed to be done should he not return home.

He started with a lengthy letter to Richard Varick, who as his lawyer would handle Calvin's will and would resolve any business affairs, including the sale of the firm.

His letter to Katharine proved harder to compose. He wondered what she would think of his explanation for joining Barnabas. Would she see that his friendship with Judah required it? Or would she curse him for a stupid and uncalled for sacrifice? His death, no matter its cause, would leave Katharine a widow once again, forced to start her life over. He finished his letter to her with words of affection and love. If Katharine ever read them, he knew that they would be cold comfort, but he felt better having written them down.

O'Shea frowned when Calvin handed the letters to him and explained the circumstances under which they should be posted to New York.

"I know what Mr. Hardwick proposes to do," O'Shea said. "His plan to free the girl. I know that you have volunteered to take Judah's place. It's madness, if you ask me."

"Judah feels honor-bound to go himself. Would he even last a week with the exertions of a trip in this weather?"

"He may not last a week at rest here in Cincinnati," O'Shea said. "He's a very sick man."

"That is besides the point. Barnabas is resolved on going. I offered to take Judah's place."

"I hope that you have weighed the benefits against the costs. You're no adventurer, Mr. Tarkington. It's not too late to talk some sense into Mr. Hardwick."

"He will not alter his course. He loves the girl. I would do the same, if I felt as he did. Barnabas has agreed to my conditions—we will avoid a confrontation with Todd, and after we free Flavia, we will expeditiously return here."

"Do you remember your Virgil? *Dis aliter visum*. We can desire a given outcome, but if the gods have decreed otherwise, our hopes will come to naught. I'm a student of human nature. There's plenty to study, even in this remote place. Perhaps because of the location, it attracts a variety of men: 'A laird, a lord, a piper, a drummer, a stealer of beef.' Barnabas Hardwick is headstrong and reckless."

"That may be so. But I believe that I can temper his recklessness. He desperately wants the girl back. He won't do anything rash that will jeopardize that."

"I hope that is the case. I have no appetite to mail these letters of yours."

"A Chinese soothsayer once claimed that I would live to a ripe old age. I'll do nothing on this trip to jeopardize that fortune."

"You've been to China, have you?" O'Shea slapped Calvin on the back. "By God, I've read about the wonders of the Celestial Empire. I must hear your stories of the place. I insist that you return to Cincinnati in one piece so that you can relate them."

"Done," Calvin said. "I promise you a full account of the glories of

Peking, the Imperial capital, when I return. It's a promise I fervently hope to keep."

FIFTEEN

There was a keen, raw beauty to much of Kentucky. As they made their way southeast towards Mount Sterling, Calvin was struck by the variety of the terrain, as it alternated between rocky high ground, sometimes with sheer cliffs and long ridgelines, and then rolling valleys. There was scant evidence of the hand of man at work, just the occasional farm that had been carved out of the wilderness.

Game abounded, even with the hint of winter in the crisp air and strong breezes that rushed through the trees, most now nearly bare of leaves. He spotted deer—a doe and its fawn startled by their arrival—wild turkeys, raccoons, hares, squirrel, and in the woods the paw prints and droppings of what Barnabas said was a small pack of timber wolves.

Twice they came across the faint tracks of a black bear. Barnabas pointed out the markings of the bear's five toes—the claws didn't show—and explained that it was hard to track bear. Despite its massive size, such a bear walked flat-footed and didn't leave much of an imprint on the ground despite weighing several hundred pounds. Barnabas shook his head in regret: he would have preferred to hunt bear, rather than tend to the difficult business that had brought them to Kentucky.

They skirted the towns and occasional settlements on their way, detouring from the main Lexington road when necessary. They did not want to answer questions or raise any suspicions, especially as they neared Edgemont Hall. It was possible that George Todd had taken the sheriff into his confidence; for all they knew the countryside might be on the lookout for the arrival of strangers.

If questioned, they would claim to be contract hunters, headed to Lexington where they had friends waiting for them. It was a flimsy story, but Calvin was convinced that if it was told with the proper casualness by Barnabas, it would suffice.

They stopped for a meal in a clearing where much of the forest floor was covered with pine needles. Pearce and Barnabas went hunting on foot while Calvin and Cicero built a fire and attended to the horses. When Pearce and Barnabas returned with several rabbits, Cicero soon had a stew bubbling in their one battered pot.

They ate the stew with slices of cornbread. When they had finished, Barnabas boiled water and produced a small cache of tea and a few wooden cups. He, Cicero, and Calvin each had a cup of tea. Pearce laughed and produced a flask of whiskey, taking a long swig.

"Didn't know ye were so dainty," he said to Barnabas. "Drinkin' tea. Don't do much for a man on a cold night."

"I want a clear head in the morning."

"Don't worry 'bout me." He looked over at Calvin. "I been wantin' to ask. D'ye have the stomach for it, Tarkington, if it gets rough?"

"We won't let it get rough." It was Barnabas. "We're not going to put Flavia at risk."

"Let him answer," Pearce said.

"I'll do what's needed," Calvin replied.

"Will ye, now?" Pearce stared at him, the challenge explicit.

"I don't look for trouble," Calvin said. "But I don't run from it, either."

"Have ye kilt a man before?"

"You've had too much whiskey," Barnabas said. "I trust Calvin will do as he says."

Calvin's jaw tightened. "I'll answer him. Yes, I've killed men. At close quarters. I'm not proud of it, and I killed only when I had to, when it was my life or theirs. For what it's worth, I regret that I had no other choice."

"Would never have thought that," Pearce said. "Ye bein' from the city, a gentleman and such."

"You'd do well not to judge a man hastily," Calvin replied. "In turn, I'll not judge you a reckless man, despite what you've said. I hope my estimation is correct, for I have no wish to die because of another man's foolhardy recklessness."

* * *

The terrain changed as they rode further south. They skirted the Knob Hills, now to the east, and entered a series of valleys which broadened into a long plateau of open pastures and rich fields, many covered with long grass that still retained some green, a verdant landscape even in the diffused early light.

Edgemont Hall was located between Mount Sterling and Winchester, the region's two small market towns. Since Barnabas had made the trip before, he kept an eye out for landmarks. When they reached a small ridge and spotted, in the distance, a large white structure, Barnabas announced that it was Edgemont Hall. They tethered their horses to some nearby trees.

"How close are we?" Calvin asked.

"A few miles, if I had to guess," Barnabas said. "It may be further because we're on high ground. When we brought Flavia and Pompey away, we struck due northeast to reach the hills. We knew that Todd and his men could catch us in the flatlands if we headed directly for Cincinnati. Todd was more clever than we thought—or he had someone who could track well—because he went to the northeast and arrived before us."

There was a classical flair to Edgemont Hall, four white Corinthian columns in the front of the red-brick main house, and two symmetrical wings, with matching smaller columns on either side of the residence. Situated behind the main house was a large unpainted barn and stables, and several smaller structures, which Calvin imagined, might be slave quarters. Blue smoke rose into the sky from the chimney of one of the buildings. Three or four horses were visible in a fenced-in corral near the barn.

The main house had been built after the threat of Indian attack had passed; an owner concerned about raiding parties would never have placed so many windows to defend in the main house, and there were several stands of trees within rifle range where attackers could hide.

Calvin had a moment of regret: there was an ordered peacefulness to Edgemont Hall that he admired. He knew that their arrival would disrupt that harmony. It was hard to make the connection between what George Todd had countenanced at Canaan, and the scene before them.

"It is an impressive place, is it not?" Calvin asked.

"Do not forget that it was built on the backs of their slaves," Barnabas said. "Directly and indirectly. Todd and his ilk should remember Toussaint L'Ouverture and his revolutionaries."

Calvin shook his head, rejecting the notion. He had heard the stories about the violent slave uprising in the French colony of Saint-Domingue.

"I shudder at the thought of a slave revolt in America," Calvin said. "The loss of life, the atrocities. It would be put down, eventually, with even more gruesome consequences."

"Either you're free or you're not," Barnabas said flatly.

"The vast majority of slaves would not be prepared for immediate freedom. They would be lost. Gradual manumission is a much better way."

"Better for whom? Not for the slaves. Every day they wait is another day spent in bondage."

"The law must be changed."

"But will it? You're here to help me steal another man's property, yet you know that it's just. If Flavia deserves freedom, doesn't every other slave?"

"Ye can jaw all day and night," Pearce said. "Time's a wastin'. I say we catch 'em with their britches down and git her now."

"We must scout them out, first," Barnabas said. "Cicero will come with me. You can wait here with Calvin."

"Suit yerself, Barnabas," Pearce said. "Just don't get shot, 'cause I ain't carryin' ye back to Cincinnati." He grinned at the thought.

"We'll return within the hour or so," Barnabas said.

"How will we know if you've run into trouble?" Calvin asked.

"Cicero is confident that we can stay out of sight. We'll take no risks."

"If you are found out, what do you propose we do?" Calvin asked.

"We'll return here as fast as we can. Have the horses saddled, and be at the ready to provide covering fire. God forbid it comes to that."

SIXTEEN

New York

Later, Katharine remembered those late autumn weeks as a quiet, unhurried time, a time of reflection and of anticipation. She was counting the days until Calvin's expected return—sometime before Christmas, or perhaps later?—while conscious that she was soon to give birth, to become a mother. She felt her body changing, thickening, as her child grew, and she marveled at the new life inside her. She had begun to show, and Tabitha had to let out several of her dresses.

To help pass the time, she ransacked Calvin's library for interesting books, rereading many of Shakespeare's plays and marveling, once again, at John Donne's poetry. She tried some of Calvin's favored Roman and Greek philosophers in the few translations he had acquired but found them slow going.

Tabitha took care of the cooking and cleaning, and so Katharine had few duties around the house. She turned to another distraction, spending an hour or so every day playing the spinet that had been stored in one of the upstairs bedrooms. Katharine found sheet music from a London publisher for several piano sonatas and practiced them until she could play them by heart. It had been years since she had played any musical instrument, and she was delighted to find that she remembered the fingering for the chords she had learned years ago.

She had time to think, to reflect. She decided that when Calvin returned she would tell him about her past, confess her shame at having lied to him, and ask for his forgiveness. She believed that he would understand.

She was less sure whether she should reveal her dealings with Devlin Phelan. She struggled with what to do. She despised Phelan and his unwelcome presence in her life, and part of her wanted him called to account for blackmailing her. Yet she recognized the risk in telling Calvin. If he confronted Phelan, there was no way of knowing what might happen, and it would most likely expose her, and Calvin, to nasty gossip.

She finally decided it would be best if she remained silent about Phelan blackmailing her.

One chilly afternoon, she was playing a light sonatina when Tabitha knocked on the door to announce that Livingston Rhodes had arrived.

"Was that you on the spinet?" Livingston asked when she came into the drawing room.

"It's been years," she said. "I pray it wasn't too discordant."

"It was delightful." He hesitated, weighing his words. "Sarah played, you know. The spinet was meant as a wedding present. After she was gone, Calvin couldn't bear to see it every day in the drawing room as a reminder of what he lost, but he also wouldn't sell it."

"I did not know the history. Calvin never said anything." She looked down. "Perhaps I should not play it."

"On the contrary, you *should* play. You must make this your house. Banish the ghosts. Better for Calvin. Better for you. What's past should be past."

She decided to change the subject. She was not eager to discuss the past. "What's happening in the world, Livingston?"

He shook his head. "Sadly, there's word of a failed invasion of Ireland by the French."

"An invasion? When?"

"The end of August. Napoleon's General Humbert landed at Killala Bay in Connacht. It looked promising at first. They routed the Loyalists at Castlebar, but the United Irish in Dublin didn't rise. In the end, a sorry, sorry affair. Lord Cornwallis caught up to Humbert at Ballinamuck on the eighth day of September. It was a slaughter."

"The same Cornwallis who was at Yorktown?"

"The very same. Charles Cornwallis."

Katharine shook her head. "You say that the leaders in Dublin did not call for another rising, even with the French on the march?"

"They did not. The Protestant gentry and barristers were more worried about losing their position to the Catholics if the French succeeded than they were in freeing Ireland. Tone didn't accompany General Humbert. Still in Paris, I would think."

Katharine sighed. "After all the sacrifices that have been made, to hear of another failure." She frowned. "The news is disheartening."

"The supporters of the cause are not taking it well," Livingston said. "I ran into that nasty man Devlin Phelan at the Bull's Head. He's still in the city. He was in his cups and quite angry over the news. Angry at the world."

"A horrid man," she said.

"He asked about you, Katharine, but I moved to cut the conversation short. I know you don't care for him."

"Thank you. I had only the most tenuous connection with him in the past, and then only through Sean. I can only hope to avoid him in the future."

"We are in firm agreement on that."

* * *

After Livingston's departure, she sat alone in the drawing room with a cup of tea and thought about the news he had related. It was clear to her that the failure of the summer rising and the French intervention had been a significant blow to any hopes for Irish independence. The death of Lord Fitzgerald, and Theobald Wolfe Tone's isolation in France, meant there was little immediate hope of overthrowing British rule.

She had hoped that Devlin Phelan might leave New York and join the Irish revolutionaries in France, or even journey to Ireland and enlist with the rebel forces. She doubted that he would depart America, now that the rising had failed. Sean had once told her that Phelan was very cautious when it came to his own skin.

Katharine was not surprised when she gazed out the front window and spotted Phelan shambling up Greenwich Street, clearly drunk. It was clear to her that he was coming to see her.

She went to the kitchen and found Arnold Hopkins there, contentedly smoking a clay pipe and watching his wife make a pie crust, and asked him to be prepared to join her in the drawing room.

"I'm expecting a caller," she told him. "A crude man, of the sort we discussed. He may even be drunk. I feel obliged to hear him out, but I would like you nearby. I will call for you if there's a need."

Hopkins bobbed his head in acknowledgment. "I'll be ready, ma'am. Say the word."

She waited by the front door, and opened it at the first knock. Phelan stood on the stoop, swaying slightly.

"Lucky Kate," he said. "Have you heard the hard news from home?"

"This is my home, now," she said.

"The French have failed us. I never believed they could be trusted. I told them, told the great Tone, that. He didn't listen."

"Why are you here?" she asked.

"Do you wish to discuss this in the street, where the world can hear us?"

She let him into the foyer, but that was as far as she would allow him to go into the house. They stood there facing each other, and she stepped back, repulsed by the smell of alcohol and sweat emanating from him.

"I'm a man of my word, Kate. Have you forgotten your debt to me? You owe me fifty dollars."

"I owe you nothing. A man of your word. A blackmailer."

"It's a small price to pay to avoid what will happen if you don't make me good. And you're a hypocrite. If you were as virtuous as you pretend to be, you wouldn't have paid me in the first place. If you won't satisfy me, I plan to tell my tale to your husband's friends." He fumbled in his coat pocket and produced a piece of folded-over paper. He wobbled slightly as he glanced at it. "I've composed a letter. It relates the past of one Kate Connaughton, formerly of Dublin and Philadelphia. I'll dispatch this letter first to Mayor Varick, one of your husband's wealthy friends. A man of rectitude, they say. I have no doubt he will share what I relate about your past with his wife, and she will tell her friends. By the time your husband returns, your reputation will be in tatters."

"Lies," she said. "No one will believe any of it."

He studied her for a moment, his eyes dropping to her waist. "You've put on weight, haven't ye? Not with child, are ye?"

"How dare you." She flushed.

"So it's true? You're blushing."

"Get out."

"How long has your husband been away? A month or two now, isn't it? Can you prove who's the father?" He stared at her. "A woman who has lied about her past. Your husband has been away. Who's been in Kate's bed?"

She glared at him, speechless.

"Your husband may believe you, or he may not," he continued, pleased with himself. "Even if he accepts your word, won't there always be doubt? You've lied to him. Infamously. How is he to know that you haven't played him false?"

"You're monstrous," she said. "A devil."

"No, I'm not. I'm simply looking to get ahead in the world. You've done well by yourself, and I'm only asking that you share your good fortune with friends."

"You're not my friend."

"I should have been. I regret that Sean watched you like a hawk when there were other men around. We could have been good friends. Always wondered what you'd be like in bed."

She glared at him. "You may be drunk, Mr. Phelan, but you've no right to say such things to me. Shall I summon Mr. Hopkins to have you put out of my house?"

"No need. I'll be off. You have two weeks to raise the money."

"Send your letter," she said. "I don't care."

"Ah, but you do, Kate. I can see it in your eyes. You don't want to lose what you have here. So I fully expect you'll pay when I return."

He stopped for a moment when he reached the doorway. "You're riding your high horse today," he told her. "When I see you next, you'll be out of the saddle. Of that I'm certain."

* * *

She didn't hesitate to send Arnold Hopkins with a message to Livingston Rhodes, asking him to come to Greenwich Street without delay. She paced back-and-forth in the drawing room, anxious and depressed by the turn of events.

"Have you had word from Calvin?" Livingston asked when he arrived. "Is all well?"

"No word," she said. "I asked you to come for a different reason. I'm in trouble, and I need your help. I should have confided in you earlier, but I was ashamed."

"Ashamed?" He shook his head, his spectacles flashing. "Absurd. What on earth could you have to be ashamed of?"

"I have not been truthful. Not with you, nor with Calvin. The day we encountered Devlin Phelan on the Bowling Green, I feared that my past had caught up with me, and it had." She took a deep breath. "Phelan knows that I was never married to Sean Daly. I lived with Sean as his wife, but there was never a ceremony, civil or religious. Phelan is blackmailing me with this fact, threatening to tell Calvin's friends that I'm no better than a kept woman."

"And Calvin? Does he know?"

"He does not. I didn't want him to think less of me, Livingston." She fought back tears. "I know what it looks like—that I deliberately deceived him, that I wanted him to think I was a widow, not a fallen woman. It's not like that."

Livingston nodded. "There's some who would think that. It's difficult enough for a widow without means of her own to remarry." He squinted at her. "I don't think your prior status would have troubled Calvin a whit. What will bother him is that you did not tell him the truth on a matter of personal significance."

"If I could change that, if I could turn the clock back, I would tell him everything. If I lost him because of it, it would be better than how I feel. The dread I feel. Carrying his child and yet imagining the worst between us when he returns."

"This man Phelan. You say he has threatened you. To what end?"

"He has asked for money. And, he has made crude advances on me. Phelan says he will go to Calvin's friends and tell them about Sean and other things, horrible lies. Mr. Hopkins and his wife are at Greenwich Street with me because I wouldn't feel safe alone in this house without them here."

"Have you paid him anything?"

She looked down at the carpet, avoiding his eyes. "I have. I've been a fool. He asked for one hundred dollars in silver to stay silent, and I gave him fifty in the hopes that he would leave me alone. Of course, we pretended it was to support the cause. Now he wants another fifty. He came here today to demand it. What's worse is that he guessed that I am with child, and threatened to spread rumors that Calvin wasn't the father if I didn't pay."

"He's devilish," Livingston said. "As wicked as he's clever. But not clever enough, I think." He adjusted his spectacles. "I believe that there is a way to end his scheme swiftly and quietly."

"How, Livingston? What if he spreads these stories? Even if Calvin believes me, forgives me, what about our place in New York? His wife will have a blackened reputation."

"His true friends will not turn their backs," Livingston said. "And don't be fooled by the prim and proper facades of New York's best. You would be surprised at the stories that could be told about their pasts."

"And our child? I can't bear the idea that our son or daughter would ever learn of this."

"With what I have in mind, they never will." Livingston smiled grimly. "We must silence Phelan and force him to leave New York. I have some ideas about how we might do that. And when Calvin returns, you must decide what you will tell him. I would advise that you hold nothing back."

"I'm very worried, Livingston. I can't stand this."

"We have two weeks. If we need more time, we can send Phelan a note saying that you've changed your mind and that you'll have the money for him on a date certain in the future. He'll wait."

"What is your idea?"

"It's not fully formed, but it's Shakespearean in design, if I may say so. I'll call again in a few days, and we can commence."

* * *

Livingston was as good as his word. Two days later, he arrived on her doorstep, as promised, but with a young woman in tow. He smiled at Katharine's confusion.

"This is Jenny," he said. "She'll help you around the house during the day. With you getting closer to having the child, you need an extra set of hands. I'm sure Tabitha will appreciate the assistance."

Jenny curtseyed and murmured something. She was tall, Katharine's height, with long red hair and a plain face. "Pleased to meet you, ma'am," she said.

"This arrangement with Jenny will be temporary," Livingston said. "Until certain matters are resolved. I took the liberty of introducing her to Mrs. Hopkins the other day, so all should go smoothly."

Once Jenny had left the drawing room to join Tabitha in the kitchen, Katharine confronted Livingston.

"Why have you brought her here?" she asked. "I'm mystified by this. What does this girl have to do with your plan?"

"Patience, Katharine. As you know, I yield to no man in my love of Shakespeare. Jenny will play a special role in our little comedy."

"Comedy? I don't understand."

"A comedy, because virtue will triumph and there will be a happy ending. When the time comes, Jenny's value will become quite evident."

"What time is that?"

"When you invite Phelan here to Greenwich Street to collect his money. I'll deliver a message to him, implying that you'll be alone, that Arnold, your manservant, is away. When Phelan arrives here, it will be Jenny who receives him, not you, but she'll make sure he can't see her face clearly. In his drunken state, he may mistake her for you and make advances. She'll resist, and a few of us will intervene. Forcefully."

"What if he doesn't fall for it?"

"We'll seize him anyway, and quite fortuitously discover a bag filled with Tarkington silver and jewelry on his person. Then, we can have him charged with theft if he won't abandon his current course."

"Will this work?" she asked skeptically.

"I'm counting on Phelan's greed and lust. One way or the other he'll fall into the trap. To preserve your reputation, you must not be directly involved in this. There is more to my plan, but it's best that I keep you in the dark about all of its facets."

"Livingston, what you have described strikes me as a very risky scheme."

"Bold, not risky. If we fail, you're no worse off than before. If it works, you won't have to worry about Devlin Phelan. We must move quickly and boldly to resolve this."

She nodded. "Bold it is, then."

PART FIVE

SEVENTEEN

Kentucky

The girl lies on the pallet, alone in the half-dark. She stares at the whitewashed ceiling above her. She can see it clearly in the moonlight, looming above her, a pale, blank space, and she wishes that somehow she could float up through the air and disappear into its whiteness, to be embraced by it, to be enveloped and consumed by it.

She does not sleep, for she fears that he will come that night. He is to leave for Lexington the next day, and he will want to possess her again before he goes.

All day the faces of the other servants have shown their knowledge of what is to come. When they look at her, she can feel the judgment. *He git you tonight* one of the stable boys whispers when he passes her in the kitchen. *Massa bone you good tonight.*

She ignores him, as she does Toby, who since her return has been trying to touch her and pull her away to do what he wants. She will not let him and he abuses her for it. *Bitch! You too white for me? You see when he gits tired of you. Then you spread them legs.*

When she had been given her own room in the main house, she knew what it meant. She understood the looks she had been getting from Bessie and Ruby and the others—some of pity, some of jealousy, some of indifference.

Now many of the other women in the house shun her. She believes that some are jealous of the light color of her skin and the softer texture of her hair. Now, she is their Master's favorite. It is not of her doing, but that doesn't seem to matter.

He has visited her repeatedly since their return, coming into the room without hesitation. After all, he regards it as his right—he is making use of his property—and what could she do? It is not her fault. She says that to herself: *not my fault.* But she feels ashamed and somehow responsible. *Not my fault.*

It had begun on the return trip to Kentucky. On the first night, when they made camp, he had the men pitch a tent. He told her to sleep there, hidden from sight, and she had not been surprised when he crawled into the tent once night fell. She had tried to fight him off, but he had slapped her hard in the face, twice. Tears had come to her eyes, and her cheek had smarted where he had hit her, but she did not cry out. He had told her harshly that she was his, and that he would have her whenever he wanted.

In the morning, she had hated the sly way the other men had looked at her at first, the muttered lewd comments and, then, when his back was turned, the hungry stares, the whispered invitations.

The second time, she did not fight. She lay there and let him have her, without moving, almost without breathing, keeping her eyes squeezed tightly shut. Afterward, she felt dirty, ashamed of what she was forced to do, even though she had no say in the matter. *Not my fault. Not my fault.*

It had been the same routine, the same pattern since. He could not leave her alone.

She knows he will whisper to her tonight as he kisses her face and neck and touches her body, tracing the curve of belly and thighs with his hands. He will tell her how he thinks about her and burns for her during the day, how he cannot wait until nightfall to come for her.

She says nothing in return, and speaks only when he threatens her if she does not. *Say my name,* he will command. *George Todd. My master.* Say it. She says it, without inflection, wishing that she had the will to resist. Over his shoulder, she stares at the ceiling, trying to lose herself in its blank whiteness. She is glad on the nights when the moon is bright, for she will be able to see the ceiling from its reflected light and try to lose herself in it.

She is ashamed that her body responds to his touch in any way, that she cannot control all her responses, some that seem beyond her control. It confuses her that a man she loathes so can somehow reach her, connect with her, even when she hates him.

Most of all, she prays that she will not bear his child.

She remembers the whispers when she first came to the house as a young girl, the talk about her pale skin and straighter hair. Some of the others had wondered out loud about her connection with the old master—had she been the product of one of his couplings? She could not believe that. If it were so, then she was even further lost—for it made her guilty not only of the sin of fornication, but of lying with her half brother.

She wonders what Missus Eleanor thinks. Does she hate her? It is common knowledge that Missus Eleanor has not been able to bear a child—not that they haven't tried. Sally, one of the Todd's oldest servants, had told them all about the arguments in their master's bed chamber.

She has lost hope. She sees how closely she is watched. She does not think that there is any escape. Flint is dead. Barnabas is a hundred miles or more away, in the Northwest country, and he might be as well be on the moon.

Her time in Canaan seems like a dream, a time when she had begun to believe that she was free of Edgemont Hall. In Canaan, she had experienced kindness and respect for the first time. There, she had fallen in love.

She thinks about Daniel Flint, and how he was always praying. He always tried to get her to join him, and even when he thought she was praying, when she was on her knees with her hands clasped together, she wasn't.

But there is Barnabas. She conjures up the image of his face, the way a smile seems to hang at the edge of his lips, the way he looks at her—not like the other men. He has never tried to force himself on her, and yet she knows that he wants her. She would have given herself to Barnabas if he asked—he had stirred feelings in her that she hadn't felt before. He made her feel safe, wanted, treasured.

There is nothing he can do now. Barnabas will forget her. Why should he care about her, a slave, George Todd's whore? He will turn his back on her.

She is alone, totally alone. *Not my fault. Not my fault.*

EIGHTEEN

Kentucky

There was little time to waste, for they knew that the longer they remained in Montgomery County the more likely it was that someone would notice the presence of strangers. Barnabas and Cicero left to approach Edgemont Hall on foot. Calvin and Pearce waited with the horses in a copse of trees a mile or so from the farm. Cicero had assured them that he had a way of contacting Pappy, one of his friends, by imitating a bird call. Cicero would meet Pappy behind the Todd's small sawmill a quarter of a mile from the main farm buildings.

Calvin immersed himself in his copy of *The Enchiridion* while Pearce passed the time by whittling a piece of oak wood. They didn't have to wait for very long—Barnabas and Cicero returned within two hours.

Barnabas shook his head when he caught Calvin's eye. "No sign of Flavia," he said. "Cicero learned from Pappy that she's being kept in the main house, in an upstairs room under lock and key. When we scouted around, I counted three white men near the house, and another two by the barn."

"Do they appear to be on guard?" Calvin asked.

"They do. All carry rifles, even when they are doing their chores. They're prepared for an attack."

"What about Todd?" Pearce asked.

"Massa Todd not dere," Cicero said. "He gone to Lexington. Pappy don't say when he come back."

"Did your friend believe Flavia could steal away from the house?" Calvin asked. "Could she make her way to the woods?"

Cicero grimaced. "Dey watch Flavia. All de slaves been tole to watch."

"I say hit 'em at first light," Pearce said. "Surprise 'em. Grab the girl and run for it."

"Against the five men guarding the farm?" Calvin asked. "Even if we retrieved Flavia, we'd raise the entire countryside against us. We'd have half of Montgomery County in pursuit."

"I agree with Calvin," Barnabas said. "We need to take care in how we do this. I don't doubt that we can free her, but that only gets us half the way there. We need to get out of Kentucky."

"The girl ain't gone to free herself," Pearce said. "Ain't it up to us to git her?"

"George Todd's absence offers us an opportunity," Calvin said. "We may be able to resolve this peacefully." He looked over at Barnabas. "Let me approach Mrs. Todd. I think that she'll listen to me. I'll explain the situation, tell her about Canaan, about the possibility of murder charges being brought against her husband in Cincinnati."

"Tarrant refused to issue a warrant," Barnabas said.

"She doesn't know that. She'll grasp how damaging it would be to have her husband publicly connected with Black Turtle and the killing of the Flints. She can prevent that if she'll release the girl. I'll offer to purchase Flavia, at a more than fair price."

Barnabas frowned. "I don't think it will work."

Pearce grunted in disbelief, and spat on the ground dismissively. "Bad idea. We should go in at dawn and git the girl."

"A direct assault could be costly," Calvin said. "And as soon as the first shot is fired, we've placed the noose around our necks in the eyes of the authorities. There's no guarantee that an attack will succeed, and then what?"

"You hardly know this woman," Barnabas replied, his jaw set. "You had one conversation with her in Maysville. Do you believe that you can convince her? Even if you did, she can't sell her husband's property without his permission."

"She's a proud woman. I believe that she'll see this as a chance to rid herself of her husband's concubine. Who cares if the sale is properly legal or not, as long as Flavia departs Edgemont Hall?"

"Cain't surprise 'em if ye go in there stirrin' things up," Pearce said. "They'll know that we're here."

"I don't plan to share the knowledge of your presence with her," Calvin said. "If Eleanor Todd refuses to release Flavia, I'll tell her that I'm returning to Cincinnati. Then we can decide what to do."

"I'm here to get Flavia," Barnabas said. "I say that we let Calvin try to convince Todd's wife. If he fails, then we go in and take her by force."

* * *

Calvin left his long rifle behind at their makeshift camp, and rode slowly down the long road that led to Edgemont Hall. When he passed the empty gate house and neared the main entrance, he hoped that he appeared to be nothing more than a solitary visitor to George Todd's estate.

Calvin dismounted from his horse and tied the reins to the ring on the hitching post. There was a carved pineapple—the traditional symbol of hospitality—displayed over the front doorway. Calvin took a deep breath to steady himself, and then rapped the brass door knocker to announce his presence.

He doffed his English slouch hat as he waited for the door to open. When it did, a pretty Negro slave appeared to greet him. Her skin was darker than Flavia's in color, but it was clear that she had some white blood. Calvin had heard that many of the owners chose the better-looking slaves to serve as house servants.

He stepped into the front hall, a large room with painted wooden wall panels, and a thick, throw rug. Eleanor Todd appeared a moment later, smiling broadly and extending her slim hand in welcome when she recognized him.

"This is a surprise, Mr. Tarkington," she said. "A pleasant surprise to find you here, dressed like a frontiersman. Weren't you planning to return directly to New York?"

"I was. My plans have been altered. I've come here from Cincinnati on a matter of some urgency." He lowered his voice. "It concerns your husband."

"George is not here," she said. "He's in Lexington, on business. Could I be of help?"

"That will depend," Calvin said. "May we talk in private?"

She led him into a large drawing room, a puzzled look on her face. Calvin glanced around at the red upholstery on the low-back sofas; the fabric was Bingham damask, one of Sarah's favorites.

They sat in elegant dark wooden chairs. The early afternoon light cascaded through the crystal glass windows surrounding them. "What is this matter of urgency?" she asked.

"I've come here from a settlement in Ohio called Canaan," Calvin began. "I'm here in the hopes of a remedy, of sorts, for an injustice. Your husband led an expedition into the Northwest country three weeks ago in search of runaways."

She waved her hand in the air dismissively. "I'm aware of that. He returned with the servant Flavia, and we were all pleased to have her restored to us."

"Yet to accomplish that restoration, your husband and his confederates killed a man named Daniel Flint and his son Micah. In concert with a party of Shawnee, they raided the settlement called Canaan, and seized Flavia."

Eleanor Todd gasped. "How dare you come into my house and make these outrageous charges, sir? How dare you?"

"These charges are true," Calvin said.

"I don't believe you."

"What did your husband tell you about Flavia's recovery?"

She remained silent, her face a pale mask.

"I've no reason to lie," Calvin said. "I regret that I'm the one to inform you."

She looked away from him for a long moment, and when she returned his gaze there were tears in her eyes. "I would rather know the truth. Even if it is unpleasant. I know that when George is provoked to anger, he can act rashly. Tell me why you have come here? To what end? Revenge?"

"I seek resolution. If your husband stands trial in Cincinnati, the world will know that he recruited Shawnee to kill white men. It will come out in court and he will deny it, of course, but there will be enough evidence to damage his reputation. I won't deny that it will be hard to convict your husband on the charges. But his name will be blackened."

"George would never agree to a trial in Cincinnati, nor could anyone compel him to appear."

"A warrant for his arrest on the charges of murder. Handbills offering a reward circulated up and down the river. Would not that destroy his reputation as quickly as any trial?"

"What is it that you want?"

"The girl. She must be freed without delay. Today."

She frowned. "Do you covet her as well? Is that it? You're here because you desire her?"

"I do not covet her."

"Truly? Most men do. She has been a plague on this house since the day my husband inherited her from his father. She has bewitched George. He could think of nothing else but getting her back."

"I have no personal interest in the girl. I wish to see her freed. I will concede that your husband may never face judgment or punishment for what he did at Canaan. Restoring Flavia's freedom may be the closest we can get to justice, Mrs. Todd. That's why I'm here."

"And it will wound George grievously. That's your reason, isn't it?"

He ignored the question. "If you'll let us take her away from Edgemont Hall, we'll not bring charges against your husband. What's more, I'm willing to compensate you monetarily for your loss."

She laughed bitterly. "My husband would never sell her. Not now. It's a matter of principle."

"A matter of principle?" Calvin arched his eyebrows. "Let us not mince words. The girl has become his Bathsheba. You can't want her here under your roof. Let me purchase her, and we'll take her east, far away from Kentucky. I'm from Boston. We'll send her there—where no judge or jury would return her to bondage."

"You ask me to betray my husband?"

"No, I ask you to right his wrong. In part. Do you wish the girl to remain here? By your own words, a constant temptation?"

"We should never have left Virginia," she said. "The life was so civilized there, Mr. Tarkington. When we had dances, they would bring the looking glasses down from the bedrooms so the candles would reflect the light and make the parlor as bright as day. We would dance all night—minuets, reels, country dances—and when it grew too late, we would all sleep a few hours; the women, in one room, like sisters, the men in another. Then a country breakfast and the farewells, and the carriage rides home."

Calvin wouldn't let her evade his question. "You must decide, Mrs. Todd."

"I do not wish her to remain here."

"Then rid yourself of her. Sell her to me."

She hesitated, weakening. "We are debtors, Mr. Tarkington. As we speak, my husband seeks a loan in Lexington, so that we won't lose Edgemont Hall. We are debtors, in need of funds." She paused. "I will sell you the girl for six hundred dollars."

"A queen's ransom."

"The sum must be sufficient to convince my husband that I have acted in our best interests," she said. "I can reason with him, keep him from pursuing you as I know his instincts would have him do."

"I'll need a bill of sale."

"You shall have one," she said. "Signed by George Todd."

"Include the man Cicero," Calvin said. "A bill of sale for him, as well."

"Very well. Five hundred for him. Cicero is a seasoned hand. He would fetch that much or more in New Orleans."

He was not going to haggle with her over the price. To do so would suggest that he accepted the notion of assigning a dollar value to a human. "Done. I can give you five hundred in silver, now, and a draft on the Bank of New York for the remaining six hundred."

"Have you thought about the irony of this, Mr. Tarkington? That you will become a slave owner?"

"In name only," Calvin said. "I shall promptly free them when we reach New York."

She rose to her feet, gesturing for him to follow her, and led him into a large library. It had been built in a strange, octagonal shape and was dominated by floor-to-ceiling bookshelves, filled with leather-bound books of all sizes and shapes. Two large chairs positioned near the room's large bay windows sat on a thick gray rug opposite a small writing table. Sconces around the room had well-used candles. On a shelf over the doorway, Calvin recognized a bust of Julius Caesar.

She walked over to a writing desk and, after locating several sheets of paper, sat down and carefully wrote out two bills of sale and handed them to Calvin. In turn, he gave her the five hundred dollars, and wrote out a draft on Tarkington & Scott for the remaining sum.

"I have done the right thing," she said. "Does this redeem me, then, in your eyes, Mr. Tarkington?"

"It's not for me to judge you."

"It matters to me what you think. The opinion of a man like you. Cultured, educated...." She stopped.

He shook his head. "If you are looking for an absolution, of sorts, I cannot grant it. Listen to your conscience, your inner voice. What does it say?"

"I'll get the girl," she said. "Please wait for us in the front hall."

* * *

Calvin tried to remain patient as he stood in the front hall, waiting, glancing now and then at his watch. He was eager to leave Edgemont Hall. It was thirty minutes before Eleanor Todd led Flavia down the main staircase. Flavia wore a light jacket over her dress, and she carried a small bag. Calvin wondered what Eleanor had said to her.

Flavia gave Calvin a half-smile when she reached the front hall. "Is Mr. Barnabas with you?" she asked. "Where is he?"

"I will take you to him," he told her. "He's nearby, waiting for you."

"Thank God," she said. "Thank you."

They followed Eleanor Todd through the main door to the outside. A burly white man stood by Calvin's horse and gave them a puzzled look. "Begging your pardon, ma'am, but we was told that Flavia wasn't to leave the house."

"Mr. Carvey, Mr. Tarkington has been so kind as to purchase Flavia from us for a quite handsome amount. They will be departing Edgemont Hall now."

"Mr. Todd gave me orders," the man said. "The girl was to stay in her room 'til he got back."

"I'm well aware of that. Things have changed. Mr. Todd will be pleased with the arrangement I've made."

Carvey didn't say anything in response, but stared at Calvin and Flavia.

Calvin helped Flavia onto his horse, and then joined her. Eleanor Todd stood next to them, her hand on the reins. "I would advise that you not dally in Kentucky," she said quietly. "For your good, and my good."

Calvin touched the brim of his hat. "Thank you for what you have done," he said. "It will be for the best."

As they rode away, past the gardens with their manicured boxwood hedges, down the long sloping dirt road leading from the main house, past the gate house, Calvin wondered how George Todd would react to Flavia's departure. Would he greet it with rage? Resignation? Perhaps even relief at the hard money yielded by Flavia and Cicero's sale?

It depended on how far gone Todd was. Calvin had seen men consumed by desire for a woman before, ruled by passion, not by logic. Would Todd abuse his wife for what she had done? Would he attempt to contest Flavia's sale? Would he pursue a lawsuit? Or would he seek out and employ slave catchers, and try to find Flavia in New York?

It was nearing sundown when Calvin and Flavia reached the small campsite. Barnabas had done a good job in camouflaging the camp, for Calvin almost rode directly past it and only Barnabas' quick, low whistle stopped him.

The moment Flavia had dismounted, Barnabas took her into his arms. As she clung to him, he whispered something to her and she began to cry.

"You are safe, now," Barnabas told her.

"Well, I'll be damned," Pearce said to Calvin. "Didn't think ye could do it, but ye did."

"Boston traders are said to cut a sharp deal," Calvin said. "That was not the case today. I've an empty purse, but I do have a bill of sale for Flavia and Cicero. For all intents and purposes, they're free."

Tears ran down Cicero's face. "Free," he said. "Dat's all I wanted."

"How did you manage this?" Barnabas asked. "With Todd away on business?"

"I convinced Eleanor Todd that I needed the papers. She's far from the first wife to forge her husband's name on a legal document. Nor the last."

"Will it stand up in court?"

"She took my money. They're in debt and need the silver, and she thought the price I paid would give him pause. Once we're in New York, I'll emancipate both Flavia and Cicero, make sure they have the proper papers. In the unlikely event that Todd challenges the sale and tries to reclaim them in court, they can go to Boston."

"We kin talk later," Pearce said. He looked up at the overcast sky. "Judging from them clouds, a storm's on the way. The further we git from here, the better."

"He will come," Flavia said. She kept her arms wrapped around Barnabas. "He won't listen to Missus Eleanor. No matter what she says."

"In a few days we'll be quite far away," Calvin said. "Then we will head east. I propose that you and Cicero travel with us, with Judah and Rachel and Naomi."

"Where?" she asked.

"To Philadelphia, and then to New York. I'm fortunate in having a house large enough for many guests."

Flavia looked at Barnabas. "What about you, Barnabas? You'll come with us, won't you?"

"The invitation extends to Barnabas, of course," Calvin said quickly.

Barnabas nodded. "Thank you. There are things Flavia and I need to decide, first. Together."

"The offer remains open," Calvin said.

Pearce glanced up at the sky. "Snow's comin' soon. Best to start back now, seein' as we got a long way yit to go."

NINETEEN

They rode until nightfall. Then Barnabas and Pearce built a lean-to in a clearing some seven or eight miles from Edgemont Hall. They fed the campfire all night to stay warm. The temperature stayed above freezing, but near morning it grew bitterly cold. As Flavia slept, bundled in blankets, the men took turns keeping watch. The night passed with no sign of pursuit.

They broke camp at first light, heading north on the Lexington Road, with Flavia riding with Barnabas on his big chestnut mare. Pearce dropped back to scout several times, and when he returned, he reported that the road behind them was empty of travelers.

"Ain't nobody with sense travelin'," Pearce said. "Not with a storm comin'."

"No snow yet," Calvin said.

Cicero overhead him and shook his head vigorously. "It come," he said. "Soon. I smell it. I kin tell."

When it did arrive, the snow began as a few isolated flurries, dropping down from the late morning sky and touching gently upon the land, then thickening as the storm swept in from the north. The wind picked up, rushing forcefully through the trees, a constant low whistle, stinging harshly when it whipped into their faces.

They stopped to confer just after noon. "I don't like the looks of this," Barnabas said. "We'll need to find shelter if this keeps up."

"We're not far from Bullock's place," Pearce said.

"He's a mean old bastard."

"He'd put us up for the night. A bit out of the way, but us beggars cain't be choosers."

"Hasn't he done some bounty hunting?" Barnabas asked. "Catching runaways?"

Pearce thought for a long moment. "Believe you're right. But Mr. Tarkington carries the proper papers for these niggers, and Bullock ain't stupid. He won't make trouble, being outnumbered and such."

Barnabas frowned. "We head to Bullock's. Wait out the storm."

Within minutes snow began to cascade down in a thick curtain. The ground was quickly covered with snow, and the hoof prints of their horses left only temporary marks; fresh snow quickly erased any sign of their passage.

Calvin shook off the snow that had collected on his hat. He looked to the northwest, straining to make out the landscape, and wondered whether they would be able to reach shelter at Bullock's cabin before it became too dark to proceed. Once the sun set, there would be limited visibility. At least the snowstorm would cover their tracks. By nightfall, a deepening white blanket would obscure any traces of their route.

He reached out and let the snow fall onto his bare hand. Snow was the same the world over, he decided. He remembered how a February downfall blanketed the city of Peking in China, thousands of miles from where they stood, across three oceans. What was it that the Chinese said—the stars were the same around the world?

He wondered whether it was snowing in New York. He pictured the streets of the city clean and white before horses and carriages muddied them, the street lamps once lit flickering as the evening neared. He thought of Katharine—was she watching the snow softly embracing Greenwich Street? Did it cover the bare branches of the oak and maple and occasional elm tree with a white frosting?

A sudden burst of wind, which lifted a stinging cloud of snow into his face, brought him back to his current reality.

"How much further?" he asked.

"Reckon it's another few miles," Pearce said. "As long as we don't lose the trace in this snow, Bullock's place is jus' north of here. Stayed there once. Small cabin, but it'll keep the snow off us tonight."

"How well do you know him?"

"Hunted a piece together. He likes his likker. Ornery as they come. Like I said, he ain't gonna be trouble. Besides, we'll be acrost the river tomorrow before ye kin say Jack Sprat."

* * *

Simon Bullock proved to be a far from receptive host. Pearce had ridden ahead to Bullock's cabin, and when he returned to them twenty minutes later he shook his head.

"He's a mean ole' snake," he said. "Greedy. Had to promise him a dollar to put us up fer the night. Ain't much room. It'll be a tight squeeze." He looked over at Barnabas and Flavia and smirked. "Course, some might like that."

Bullock cursed when they entered his ramshackle cabin and he spotted Cicero and Flavia. He scowled at Pearce. "Didn't say nothin' bout niggers. Don't want 'em in my house." Bullock tugged at his chin nervously. He had a bony face, and his nose looked like it had been badly broken and had healed crookedly.

"They're my servants," Calvin said. "They won't cause any trouble."

"Who are ye?"

"Calvin Tarkington."

"Ye branded that one?" Bullock asked, looking at Cicero. "Burned that mark on his face?"

"It's the letter 'T.' My name is Tarkington."

"I don't like it," Bullock said to Pearce. "Darkies bring bad luck."

"You're being paid," Calvin said. "We'll be gone in the morning."

Bullock kept his eyes fixed on Pearce. "They got that nasty nigger smell about 'em."

Pearce laughed. "They don't smell any worse than ye do, Simon Bullock. Now shut yer mouth, and cook us some supper."

* * *

The first signs of trouble came in the morning when Pearce shook Barnabas and Calvin awake. Calvin reluctantly abandoned his blankets and stood up slowly, careful not to hit his head against the low ceiling of the cabin. It was cold enough that he could see his breath.

"He's gone," Pearce said. "Simon's gone."

"When?" Barnabas asked.

"Must have been just before dawn. I don't like it one bit."

"He kept staring at Flavia," Barnabas said. "He must have seen those handbills offering the reward for her. Or he somehow heard about Todd looking for her. If he's gone to tell Todd, at least with this snow, it'll take him all day or more to reach Edgemont Hall."

"At which point, if Todd's arrived home, he'll know where we are," Calvin said. "If he's going to pursue us, this would be his chance.

Barnabas shook his head. "We must wait for the storm to let up, then we can move."

"Ain't hankerin' to freeze to death," Pearce said. "We kin fort up here. We got firewood, and we got blankets, and we got three rifles. Take turns playin' sentry, if it'll make you feel better. I reckon Todd ain't foolish enuff to come after us in this weather."

"Flavia's convinced that he will come," Barnabas said.

"He's mad if he does. A man kin lose his way in a storm like this, and the cold kin kill 'em."

"If Bullock shows him the way, Todd won't get lost," Calvin said. "I don't like the idea of being trapped here. We can only hope that Todd hasn't returned from Lexington. Bullock may find he's been on a fool's errand when he reaches Edgemont Hall."

"I ain't worried," Pearce said. "If Todd wants a scrap, he kin come here and he'll git one. Not like Canaan, that's fer sure. We'll be more than ready."

TWENTY

The snow continued to fall through the morning. At least once, Calvin had to force the door open because of the snow banked against it outside. He swept a path into the clearing with a fir branch. He estimated there was at least three feet of soft, wet snow on the ground. He couldn't see very far down the trail leading to Bullock's cabin.

They decided to take turns standing watch. Barnabas picked out a spot in a stand of pine trees that offered an unobstructed view of the cabin and its immediate surroundings.

"Probably a waste of time," Pearce offered. "They ain't comin'."

"I know how I feel about Flavia," Barnabas said. "A blizzard wouldn't stop me. Nor will it stop Todd if he learns that she's here."

"Suit yerself."

"We should prepare to make a stand here. We need to keep watching the trail."

"I'll take my turn fer now," Pearce said. "But I'd bet they ain't comin'."

"A bet I'd like to lose."

Pearce shrugged. "In the meantime, I'll go feed and water the horses. We'll be askin' a lot of 'em with this snow, once we ride out of here."

In the late afternoon, the snow turned to a hard sleet and a crust formed on the top of the snow. When Calvin took his turn at sentry duty, he found that Barnabas had stamped down the snow and cut some saplings and built a crude canopy overhead.

When Calvin returned to the cabin, he found Barnabas and Pearce in the middle of an argument. Pearce didn't want to stand watch after dark. He was convinced that, even with Bullock as his guide, Todd wouldn't attempt an attack at night.

"We been standin' out there all day wit' nothin' to show fer it," Pearce said. "I tell ye, they ain't comin'."

"What if you're wrong?" Barnabas asked. "I won't take the risk. I'll take all the watches if I need to. As long as we're in Kentucky, we can't let down our guard. Snow or no snow."

Calvin looked over from the fireplace, where he was warming himself. "Count me in. Better an abundance of caution."

Pearce cursed loudly. Calvin looked over and saw a look of concern on Flavia's face.

"Have it yer way," Pearce said. "I'll stand out there and freeze my arse. But we ain't goin' anywhere soon, nor is Todd. Them horses will have a devil of a time breakin' through that hard crust. That's a fact."

* * *

Calvin took the first watch after their hasty supper. It had stopped snowing, and a half-moon provided enough light so that he could see clearly the front of the cabin and where the trail ended in the open ground of the clearing.

A light breeze kept snow swirling about, and he draped a small piece of leather over the flintlock and pan of his long rifle to keep it dry.

His thoughts wandered as he waited, stamping his feet against the cold, keeping his eyes fixed on the trail from the south. He thought about the trip to New York. His homecoming would be quite different than he had originally imagined. Katharine would be surprised. Calvin would return with guests—Judah and his family, and Barnabas, Flavia, and Cicero. Greenwich Street would be crowded until he could get them all established and find places for them to stay in New York.

He thought there was sudden movement further down the trail, but it was hard to see through the overhanging trees. Just when he was convinced that his eyes had been playing tricks on him, he saw a dark shape and more movement.

Calvin could feel his heart beating rapidly, and he felt short of breath. He slipped off the leather piece covering the flintlock, cocked the weapon, and quickly raised his long rifle to his shoulder. He aimed for a spot well above the dark figure—he wouldn't shoot to kill unless his own life was threatened—and squeezed the trigger. The rifle shot shattered the silence. He peered through the smoke down the trail—it was empty. Whoever was there had retreated or moved into the woods.

He started reloading his rifle, cursing himself for his clumsiness—he struggled with pouring the black-grained powder from the powder horn down the barrel, then placing a ball and patch, then tamping it down with the ramrod. By the time he had finished, Barnabas had reached his side.

"I saw someone on the trail," Calvin said. "Shot over his head and scared him off."

"It has to be Todd," Barnabas said. "Flavia was right. He has come, despite the storm."

"I only saw one man. Not sure if there are more."

"I'll stay here and cover the trail," Barnabas said. "I sent Zeke into the woods to keep them from flanking us. Cicero's guarding the horses."

"Where do you want me?"

"Go back to the cabin. If Todd can get past us, that's where he'll go."

"How many men do you think he has?"

"Bullock must be with him. As for others, your guess is as good as mine."

Once inside the cabin, Calvin went to his bag and found his Bunney pocket pistol. He loaded and primed it, and was about to place it in his pocket when Flavia called over to him.

"I would like a weapon," she said. "Please, Mr. Calvin."

"Do you know how to shoot?" he asked.

"Micah let me shoot his rifle," she said. "I'm not afraid. I know I could shoot that pistol of yours."

"Are you sure?" Calvin asked.

"I'm sure."

Calvin reluctantly handed the pistol to her. He explained how she should point the weapon at her target, and then slowly squeeze the trigger. Flavia thanked him, holding the gun tightly in her right hand.

They sat in the cabin, waiting. There was only one window, and Bullock had boarded it over, so they could not see out. A few minutes later they heard several rifle shots in the distance. There was a pause, and then more shots, followed by silence, then more shots.

Calvin slipped outside the cabin and, crouching down, glanced over to where he had left Barnabas. He didn't see anyone there. From his far left, he spied two dark figures moving toward the cabin. They must have seen him, because one raised a rifle to his shoulder and fired. A shot thudded into the wall of the cabin close to Calvin.

Calvin sprinted away from the front of the cabin to a nearby oak tree where he could take cover. He pointed his rifle toward the first dark figure and squeezed the trigger. To his surprise, the gun didn't fire. He cursed—the powder must have gotten wet. As he fumbled with the flintlock, a man ran past him toward the cabin—Calvin caught a glimpse of his face and realized it was George Todd.

A moment later, another rifle fired and Calvin felt a tug on his sleeve, and realized he had been hit. He touched his arm and found a rip in his buckskins, but there was no blood. A second man had stopped some twenty yards away from him, and had begun to reload.

Calvin ran toward the man, desperate to close the distance between them before a second shot. His headlong rush rattled the man, who dropped his powder bag. Calvin clutched his long rifle by the barrel, and when he was within a few feet of the man he swung the rifle wildly. He caught him with the butt end on the side of his face, and watched as the man crumpled to the ground. Calvin stood over him, breathing heavily from the run—the man sprawling on the ground before him was Simon Bullock.

Calvin turned and ran toward the cabin, his feet slipping out from under him. He fell to the ground, gasping at the cold when he landed in the snow. He scrambled to his feet. Closer to the cabin, he heard muffled voices and an insistent male voice followed by Flavia's higher-pitched response.

He reached the door and before he could enter the cabin, was stopped short by the sound of a pistol shot. Once inside, Calvin found Flavia crouched by the fireplace, her back to the cabin wall, her eyes wide in fear. On the dirt floor, George Todd was on one knee, his hands clutched to his neck.

"By God, she shot me," he said. Blood dripped from between his fingers. "Flavia shot me."

Calvin stepped into the room and moved to interpose himself between Todd and the girl. Todd frantically tried to staunch the flow of blood with his hands. He mumbled something, and then made a strangled, hissing sound. He slumped over and fell onto the floor face down, his arms outstretched. Blood gushed out, making a pool on the dirt floor.

Calvin turned him over and saw blood flowing from an ugly throat wound. "Todd? Can you hear me?"

Todd's eyes fluttered, but there was no response. Calvin found a piece of cloth in his bag and pressed it against the wound. He heard a sound behind him—it was Barnabas, who joined him at Todd's side.

"They started shooting at me from the trail," he said. "Pulled me away from the clearing. I came back as quickly as I could." Barnabas felt for a pulse at Todd's wrist and shook his head. "He's gone." He hesitated. "You shot him?"

"Flavia did."

Barnabas moved over to the corner, where Flavia watched silently, and took her into his arms. "Thank God, you're safe," he said.

"I wouldn't go back with him," she said. "I told him that. He wouldn't listen."

"You did the right thing."

"Is he gone?" she asked anxiously.

"He is." Barnabas turned to Calvin. "We should take him outside."

Calvin lifted Todd's slim body onto Barnabas' broad shoulders, and led the way through the cabin door and out into the clearing. They placed Todd against the oak tree where Calvin had earlier sought shelter. Barnabas took his outer coat off and plunged it into the snow to wash off the blood.

Calvin looked around in the clearing and spotted Bullock's body laid out in the snow. "I knocked out Bullock," Calvin said. "He won't last long in the cold. We should take him inside."

As they were carrying Bullock to the cabin, Pearce and Cicero appeared.

"Chased a couple of Todd's men down the trail," Pearce said. "Figger they won't stop 'til they git to Lexington."

"Dey didn't come near de horses," Cicero said.

Back in the cabin, they propped Bullock against one of the walls. Pearce poured some whiskey into Bullock's mouth and he sputtered and regained consciousness.

"Where's Todd?" Bullock asked, looking around the cabin.

"Dead," Pearce said. "What ye should be, for betrayin' us to Todd the way ye did."

"How many men did Todd bring?" Barnabas asked.

Bullock stared at him sullenly. "Me, Gideon Carvey, and one other, Dan Thomas. I met them on the Lexington Road. They was already after ye. Spittin' mad Todd was, aimin' to git the girl back. Gideon didn't want to go further, 'cause of the storm, but Todd offered him and Thomas more money and they came along."

"Four men," Barnabas said.

"Todd told Carvey and Thomas to pin ye down with their rifles. Then we rushed the cabin. Todd said once we had the girl, ye wouldn't risk firin' on us. I tole him it was a mistake. Could 'ave waited ye out. Send for more men. He wouldn't listen. Had to have the girl back."

"We're going to leave you here," Barnabas said. "If you're asked about Todd, you'll say you lost him in the storm."

"He promised me silver. Never paid me."

"Your loss. Count yourself lucky. We could have left you in the snow to freeze to death. It's what you deserved."

They dug a crude grave for Todd in the woods, taking turns with Bullock's one shovel, and then piled up rocks on top of the excavated dirt in the hopes of discouraging foraging animals from digging up the body.

"How long before they come looking for Todd?" Calvin asked Barnabas when they had finished.

"A few days. Once there's less snow on the road. I suspect Bullock will lie low for a while."

"It doesn't sit well with me," Calvin said. "An unmarked grave."

"Unmarked and unfound, for now at least. Todd rode off into a winter storm. A reckless act by a reckless man. They'll reckon he froze to death and his body is somewhere in the woods. I say good riddance. He's a murderer in my book. Pompey. Daniel and Micah Flint. Three killings. He would have added us to the list. All to keep Flavia in bondage for his own twisted purposes."

"I don't think many will mourn him," Calvin said.

"What of his wife?"

"She won't shed many tears, if any. I suspect that she will quickly close this chapter of her life—sell Edgemont Hall and return to Virginia."

"Then we can rest easy? This is truly done?"

"It appears that way. How is Flavia taking it?"

"I've told her more than once that she did the right thing. Truth is, Todd never would have let her go. I believe that he would have followed us to

New York or wherever she went. To come after us in the middle of the storm was an act of madness. He was beyond reason. Only death was going to stop him."

TWENTY-ONE

The Northwest Territory

The muddy streets of Cincinnati were deserted and silent when they arrived just before dusk. There were piles of melting snow in front of some of the buildings.

Zeke Pearce bid them an awkward farewell in front of Mrs. Bainbridge's boarding house. "Ye don't have need of me now, so I'll be goin'."

"Thank you," Barnabas said. "You stood with us, as you promised."

"That I did," Pearce said. "Now to finish sellin' them bear skins and bear oil. I reckon I'll stay here for the winter, then start huntin' agin in the spring. I'll miss ye, Barnabas." He glanced over at Calvin with a sly grin. "Ye surprised me, Tarkington. Didn't think ye had it in ye, but ye did. To wallop Simon Bullock and knock him cold. A good day's work, that."

He gave Calvin a lazy half-salute, and loped up the street.

Once inside the boarding house, Calvin was surprised to find Jack O'Shea in the common room, donning his winter coat.

"I was just leaving," O'Shea said. "I've been attending to Judah. We should talk."

Calvin asked Barnabas to look after Flavia and Cicero. O'Shea walked outside, motioning for Calvin to join him. "Judah has taken a turn for the worse," he said, lowering his voice. "Can't eat. Sharp pains in the stomach. Blood in his urine. Some sort of mass of tissue in his abdomen. I remember a case like this in London." He shook his head. "The autopsy found a tumorous growth inside the body."

"A tumor? Cancer?"

"It would be consistent with his symptoms."

"Can you operate? Can you cut it out?"

"He's too weak for surgery. Even the greatest surgeon during my time at St. Thomas Hospital, John Hunter, wouldn't attempt it, and he could remove a bladder stone in under a minute. I don't believe it would do Judah any good. I've administered laudanum for his pain, and I've had to increase the dosage in the past few days for it to continue to work."

"Could he rally?"

"If my diagnosis is correct, it would only postpone the inevitable. He's dying. It may only be days."

"That's grim news."

"You recovered the girl."

"We did."

"At least you have that," O'Shea said. "Send for me if there's any change in his condition. I'll return tomorrow in the afternoon."

When Calvin returned to the boarding house, he asked to see Judah. Rachel brought him into a ground-floor bedroom. A gaunt, pale Judah lay in the bed. His skin had a pronounced yellowish tinge to it. He smiled at Calvin's greeting.

Calvin quickly related the story of their rescue of Flavia and the confrontation with Todd.

"Poetic justice," Judah said. He took a shallow breath. "Todd pays for his crimes, even if justice doesn't come from a judge and jury. Barnabas must be overjoyed to have saved Flavia."

"He's a happy man. Doesn't leave her side."

"Did you see Dr. O'Shea?"

"I did."

"I insisted that he give me his honest opinion, and it is not a promising one. I would assume that he has shared his diagnosis with you." Judah spoke slowly and deliberately. "There is no point in denying the obvious. My body has betrayed me. Why that is, I can't say. A mystery without an answer. But it means that I may not last much longer. Calvin, I've a great favor to ask of you. Under the circumstances, I have no choice but to ask now. Rachel and Naomi. They will have no one, after I'm gone. Will you watch over them?"

"I shall. You have my word."

"A long way from the Rue de Bac," he said. "Who would have thought then that we would end up here, so far away? Or that it would end for me in such a place. One other request. Please, no superstition, no talk of heaven, when you bury me. I would not have the hypocrisy."

* * *

It was clear that Mrs. Bainbridge didn't care for having Negroes under her roof, but Calvin had paid her well and so she kept to herself, ignoring them. Rachel stayed at Judah's bedside, while Flavia cared for Naomi. Barnabas and Cicero went to Burt & Newman's Saddlery, where they could sell Judah's horse. In a day or so, Calvin would purchase passage by boat to Pittsburgh for all of them with the money he had kept for the return journey.

Late in the afternoon, Jack O'Shea arrived and spent a few minutes with Judah, who had slept most of the day. O'Shea shook his head when he emerged from Judah's bedroom.

"He's barely conscious," he said. "Whether that's the laudanum, or the sickness, I can't tell. He's not breathing well."

O'Shea sat down across from Calvin, rummaged through his bag, and produced a dark-colored bottle. He poured each of them a large glass of whiskey.

"Long life and a death in Old Ireland," he said, raising his glass. Calvin drank his whiskey quickly, enjoying the warm burning sensation of the alcohol.

"You returned in one piece from Kentucky," O'Shea said. "No bullets to remove."

"I've never been shot," Calvin said. "Wounds from blades, and from an arrow. But not from a gun."

"Have you been in harm's way that often?"

"Never by choice, I can assure you. And please, call me by my Christian name. There is scant need for formality."

O'Shea smiled. "Certainly, Calvin. You chose to go with the reckless Barnabas to Kentucky. Was that the most prudent course?"

"A reluctant choice. But should an Irishman lecture on prudence?"

"You have the better of me on that. We're not the most prudent of races."

Calvin realized suddenly how tired he was. The warmth of the common room fire was making him drowsy. He hoped he wouldn't doze off in front of O'Shea.

"Another drink, Calvin?" O'Shea asked. "It's waiting for the end, now. Tell me of China and the life there. What are the people like? What of the civilization there. How does it compare?"

He poured another generous shot of whiskey for Calvin.

"The empire of Ch'ien-lung is a vast one," Calvin said. "In many ways, an advanced civilization, equal to ours." He quietly related the story of his time in China, how Calvin had been accidentally entangled in the politics of the Imperial court, and how a Manchu general had protected him and saved his life. He told O'Shea of the personalities he had encountered in Peking—the brilliant Jesuit astronomer, Father Michel, the powerful and ruthless chief minister, Ho-shen, and the cultured and lovely Lady Subai and her haunting poems.

O'Shea listened, occasionally interrupting with questions, as Calvin described the strange, and often tense, relations between Western traders and the Imperial officials. They talked deep into the night, and it was nearing one o'clock when Rachel Gomez entered the parlor. Calvin knew immediately from the look on her face that Judah had died.

"He's not breathing, Doctor," she said. "I can't rouse him. I've tried."

O'Shea rose to his feet. "I'll have a look," he said, and followed her into the bedroom.

Calvin waited in the common room. When he heard the sound of Rachel sobbing in the bedroom, he knew that Judah had commenced the final journey from which there was no return.

* * *

They buried Judah in a graveyard at the eastern edge of the town, holding a makeshift service. Dr. O'Shea had arranged for a grave to be dug, and two hired men lowered Judah's pinewood coffin into the shallow hole.

At the foot of Judah's grave, Barnabas read Psalm 16 from a borrowed Bible, and Calvin said a few words about his friend.

"I first met Judah in France, thousands of miles from here, in Paris," he began. "He joined the revolution in the hopes of establishing liberty, equality, and fraternity. And justice. It was the sad betrayal of justice that eventually caused him to leave France and come to America." Calvin turned so he could see Rachel, dressed in black, holding Naomi in her arms. "Here, he found love and companionship, and the joy of fatherhood, and here his journey came to an end. Judah would not want us to grieve for too long. He was a practical man, and he would argue that our energies were better directed in making the world a better, more just place. He was a good man, a good husband, and a good father. May he rest in peace."

Rachel and Naomi stood in the cold, mute, until the gravediggers had shoveled dirt over Judah's coffin. Calvin took Rachel's arm, and Barnabas carried Naomi, on the silent walk back to the boarding house.

Once in the common room, Calvin took Rachel aside. "Please don't worry about the future," he said. "I would propose that you and Naomi return with me to New York, just as Judah planned. There are better prospects for you there."

"Better prospects?"

"For Naomi. You must think of her, and her future."

"Where would we live?"

"My wife Katharine and I would be honored to have you stay with us. We have ample room."

"It's too much to ask," she said.

"I should be the judge of that, shouldn't I?"

Calvin knew that in the end, she would not resist the idea. Staying in the Northwest Territory would mean a bleak future. She and her child would have to depend on the charity of others, or she would have to remarry. In New York, she would have a better chance of finding a suitable husband and a step-father for Naomi. She would grieve for her loss, but in time, the pain would lessen, and the memories would fade and lose their clarity. Life would go on. How could it be otherwise?

TWENTY-TWO

New York

In the days leading up to Devlin Phelan's return visit to Greenwich Street, Katharine slept fitfully. Whenever she did doze off, she was bothered by nightmares.

In one particularly vivid dream, she found herself standing in the middle of Bowling Green, surrounded by a crowd of angry men and women. Devlin Phelan stepped forward, a malicious smile on his lips, and raised his right arm and pointed at her with his index finger. One-by-one everyone around him did the same.

Then Calvin pushed his way through the crowd and approached her. He gazed deeply into her eyes, and shook his head in disappointment with what he saw, and then turned to leave.

She cried out to him for forgiveness, but Phelan had quickly grasped Calvin's arm and was whispering into his ear, and her husband was shaking his head in dismay.

She tried to run to him, to explain, but she found herself frozen in place, unable to move. All the while Phelan kept talking, and Calvin began to cry. She felt despair, and began to cry herself.

Katharine had woken from that nightmare with a start. That morning she felt a sense of dread and foreboding. She shivered when Livingston arrived and told her that all was ready for Phelan's visit that afternoon.

"I've slept little," she told him. "A horrid nightmare the other night. Before we proceed, you must tell me more of your plan. I'm very anxious."

"It's all arranged," Livingston said. "A Mr. Billington will come by in the early afternoon. He'll wait with Arnold Hopkins and myself, and will assist us in restraining Phelan when the time comes."

"What if he resists?"

"There will be three of us," Livingston said drily. "I believe we can handle one drunken Irishman. Jenny shall wait for him in the drawing room, and in the dim light I believe he'll mistake her for you, and try to force himself on her. Moreover, there's a sack of valuables from your home—silver candlesticks, jewelry—that we'll find in his possession when we seize him. We'll be prepared to testify about how we surprised him."

"Where will I be?"

"You will wait in the library until this scene has played out."

"Won't Phelan deny it all? If he's brought before the constable, won't he try to implicate me in some way? And won't Mayor Varick be informed of the charges?"

"We don't want a trial. We want him to leave New York, and never return. We won't press charges if he does. I'll make it clear that if he ends up in court, it will be his word against that of men known for their integrity, and the word of Jenny, who will swear that he's been lurking near the house, trying to force his affections upon her."

"Jenny is willing to do this?"

"She'll be well compensated for her assistance."

"Phelan is a hateful man. Out of sheer spite, he may risk jail if he can hurt me."

"That will not be left to chance. We will swear out a criminal complaint after he's left New York. We'll make Devlin Phelan a fugitive. That means he can be arrested if he ever sets foot in New York again."

"How will you accomplish that?"

He shook his head. "There must be some mystery about this. Trust me, Katharine."

She wrote out the note to Phelan as he directed: *Come to Greenwich Street at 5 o'clock tonight. You will be paid in full. K.*

Livingston quickly left Greenwich Street carrying the message. He returned thirty minutes later. "The trap has been set," he reported. "I found Phelan at his favorite haunt, the Bull's Head, and gave him the note. I mentioned—in passing—that your servants were away for a few days and how I disliked your being left alone."

"Did he say anything?"

"He thanked me, but was otherwise silent."

"Was he drunk?"

"Drunk enough for our purposes. I'd wager Devlin Phelan is drunk enough to mistake one ginger-haired woman for another."

* * *

Livingston remained to oversee their preparations. He had them dress Jenny in one of Katharine's finer gowns, and they arranged her hair so that it fell loosely onto her shoulders.

"From a distance I would swear it was you," Livingston exclaimed to Katharine when Jenny walked into the drawing room. He positioned Jenny with her back to the front door, facing the bay window. "We want him to see your hair and your figure, but not your face."

"If he puts his damn hands where they don't belong, I'll clout him," Jenny said. "Right in his ugly snout. I know how to handle them with frisky hands."

"Don't worry," Livingston said. "We'll be ready to intervene."

Jenny gave him a puzzled look. "What's that? Intervene?"

"We'll step in and stop him as forcefully as necessary," Livingston explained.

Jenny grinned. "Not by yourself, then. You're a mite small for that. How many others?"

"Two other men. We'll wait out of sight."

Livingston instructed Kathleen to light only a few candles in the drawing room, so it would be harder to see clearly. She found herself pacing back-and-forth. At Livingston's prompting, they each drank a small glass of brandy to, as he explained it, "calm the nerves."

A few minutes before five, Katharine took up her place by the window, where she could see anyone coming up the street. When Devlin Phelan appeared, she alerted Livingston, who called for Arnold and Mr. Billington to take their place in the drawing room. Within minutes, there was a loud knock on the front door.

"Come in," Katharine called out. "I'm in the drawing room."

"Now, quickly, into the study," Livingston said. "Don't come out until I call for you." He joined Arnold and Billington in the far corner of the room, out of sight. Katharine saw that Billington, a large man with thinning hair who was dressed in a dark suit, carried an ugly-looking cudgel.

Katharine hurried into the study, leaving the door slightly ajar so she could see some of the drawing room. She heard footsteps in the foyer, and then Phelan calling her name. Then, there was silence, followed by the distinct sound of a slap, and Jenny cursing in a loud voice. Katharine heard the sounds of a struggle and then a sudden thudding noise. She quickly opened the door to the drawing room so that she could see what was happening.

She was confronted by a strange tableau—Devlin Phelan, face down on the floor, his shackled hands behind his back, flanked by Arnold and Billington. Jenny and Livingston stood by the window, and Calvin's friend wore a pleased look on his face.

"We've caught ourselves a scoundrel," he announced. "A blackguard of the worst sort."

From the floor, Phelan cursed. "Ye have no right to detain me. Let me go, or ye will pay for this, Rhodes."

Livingston didn't immediately reply. He thanked Jenny and Arnold for their help, and quietly asked them to wait in the kitchen. After they had left the drawing room, he turned his attention to Phelan.

"I'll pay nothing," he said. "On the contrary, you're the one with a bill that has come due tonight. There are consequences for burglary and assault." Livingston glanced at Billington. "If you could put Mr. Phelan on his feet."

With his hands shackled behind his back, Phelan could do little as Billington hauled him upright.

Katharine remained in the doorway to the study, where Phelan couldn't see her.

"There's been no theft, and no assault," Phelan said. "Fabrications."

Livingston held up a cloth bag. "This proves you arrived here intent on stealing valuables from the Tarkingtons." Opening the bag, he peered inside. "I see silver candlesticks and jewelry, precisely the items a thief would snatch."

"I stole nothing," Phelan said. "I came to collect a donation to the cause of the United Irishmen, promised to me by Kate Tarkington. Ye delivered the message summoning me here."

"So says you, a drunk and a rascal. And there are three of us who will swear that Jenny surprised you in the act of burglary. You attacked her, and we rushed to her assistance."

"Lies. Perjury."

"And what is the truth of this matter? You're a blackmailer, which makes you a thief. You sought to take liberties with Jenny, thinking she was Mrs. Tarkington."

"You won't get away with this. Call the constable if you dare. Have me arrested. Once in court, I'll tell quite a tale about Kate Connaughton, whore to Sean Daly, lying her way into Tarkington's bed."

"You won't tell tales to anyone," Livingston said.

"Won't I?"

"Mr. Billington will make sure of that," Livingston said, motioning toward the stranger. "You'll be seeing a great deal of him over the next few years. You'd be well served to treat him with respect."

"What's this?" Phelan looked at the stranger, confused.

"Mr. Billington is the second mate of the *Argos*, a brigantine moored at Burling Slip. It departs tomorrow for Charleston with the morning tide. You'll be aboard as an ordinary seaman."

"The hell I will."

"That choice has been made for you," Livingston said. "Your name has been added to the crew list. The shackles will stay on until you're at sea. The captain of the *Argos* is a close friend of the Tarkington family. Aboard a merchant ship, the captain is in absolute command." He stared at Phelan. "You'll keep your mouth shut tight, and will work without complaint." Livingston frowned. "It's a sad fact that men are lost at sea. Would there be any dry eyes in New York or Dublin if you were to slip overboard during a storm? To avoid such an accident, I'd suggest that you do as you're told."

"Cap'n Cushman's a fair man," Billington said. "But he has no use for sea lawyers, layabouts, and malingerers, nor do I. And I promise that we'll keep a close eye on ye."

Livingston nodded. "You'll remain aboard the *Argos* when it reaches Charleston, Phelan. From there, it's across the Atlantic and on to the East Indies. Should you manage to find your way back to America, don't set foot in New York. Tomorrow, we'll swear out statements with the high constable about tonight's episode. There will be a warrant outstanding for your arrest for burglary and indecent assault."

Katharine decided that she could wait no longer. She stepped forward into the drawing room so they could see her. "I have something to say," she began, staring at Phelan, who dropped his eyes. "For what you have done, and what you tried to do, I would have you beaten to within an inch of your life. What faces you at sea is a better punishment—a hard life for a soft city man."

"When my husband returns, he will hear the entire story. I think of him as a gentle man, but Livingston assures me that he would have no mercy on anyone who threatened his family. To be clear—never return to New York. You've been given fair warning."

"You're no better than me," Phelan said. "Making your way in the world with more than a lie or two."

"Don't you dare compare us," she said. "I concealed my past for reputation's sake, not that I have anything to be ashamed of. I regret that I was weak when I should have told you to go to hell. I've no fear of you, or of what you could say or do. As you have seen tonight, I have friends I can rely on."

Phelan didn't respond.

"There's a carriage waiting for us outside," Billington said. He prodded Phelan in the back with his cudgel. "One of my bruisers will come along to make sure ye don't try to stray. We'll go straight to the *Argos*."

Katharine waited by the window until after she had seen the carriage head down Greenwich Street with Phelan securely inside, flanked by Billington and another very large hulk of a man. Then, once she was sure he was gone, she took a deep breath.

"Thank you, Livingston," she said. "It was marvelous. You've thought of everything."

"I must say that I'm quite proud of the way it all unfolded. Phelan took the bait, responded just as I had intended. He's a rather pathetic villain, in his own way."

"I'm so glad to be free of him. It's a great weight lifted off my shoulders."

Livingston removed his spectacles, and polished them with his shirt front. "Tonight makes me wonder if I should try my hand at playwriting. A comedy, of course, just like our little entertainment."

"You might be able to call this a comedy," she said. "But it felt quite tragic to me."

Livingston put his spectacles back on and smiled at her. "Certainly a comedy. It only awaits the hero being restored to home and hearth, and his beloved and faithful wife."

"It won't be finished until I've told Calvin everything," she said. "I can't help but worry."

"Calvin has seen more of the world than most men. I'm sure he will take it all in stride."

"I wish I could be as confident. He will be disappointed, I'm sure, but I hope that the news of the baby will soften the sting."

After Livingston had left, Katharine climbed the steps slowly to the second floor. From the bay window in the bedroom, she looked out over Greenwich Street in the dwindling light, one hand gently touching her belly, ready for any movement of the child. Below her, the branches of a nearby beech tree stood bare against the winter wind.

She could hear the ticking of the English clock on the bedroom table behind her, marking the time. A dog barked in the distance. She sighed. How soon would she be reunited with Calvin? What would he think, of the baby, of the episode with Phelan? Livingston was confident that Calvin would understand, but she questioned that certainty.

They had married quickly, after all, and she couldn't claim to truly know Calvin. It had to be the same for him—in some ways, she was still a stranger to him. She didn't welcome the idea of revealing what she hadn't told him before. It promised to be an awkward, strained homecoming, one that mixed good news with bad.

TWENTY-THREE

They left Pittsburgh on New Year's Day. The wind whipped snow flurries through the air, and the muddy streets were icy in the January cold.

The evening before, Calvin, Barnabas, Flavia, Cicero, and Rachel had gathered in the large common room at Peterson's Inn to welcome in the New Year. Outside, snow fell without pause, and the wind howled against the house. They stayed warm by the blaze in the large, brick fireplace, waiting until just before midnight to sample some of the rum punch Mr. Peterson had prepared for the celebration.

As they stood in a small circle of sorts, Calvin raised his mug. "Shall we toast the New Year? And wish for a more peaceful one ahead with friends and family?"

"And for a safe journey to New York," Barnabas replied.

They raised their mugs in concert and drank deeply. Calvin was pleased that Rachel had joined them while Naomi slept soundly in a nearby bedroom. Rachel's cheeks flushed from the punch. She stayed close by Calvin's side, and he understood why—he now represented the only stability in her world, one turned upside-down.

She had spent the journey to Pittsburgh in a daze. Calvin had heard her crying quietly in the night, once Naomi was asleep. When Rachel wasn't attending to her daughter, she had been silent, morose and glum. She had picked at her food, and Calvin worried about her health. He hoped things would improve for her when they reached New York.

Barnabas kept one arm around Flavia's waist, and put his mug down on a nearby table. "An announcement, if you please. After we reach New

York, after Flavia becomes a free woman, we'll be married. And Flavia has chosen a new name."

"Faith," she said. "I wish to be called Faith. After we wed, I'll be known as Faith Hardwick. A new name for a new life."

"It's a lovely name," Calvin said. "My heartiest congratulations. Once we're in New York, Katharine will want to help with the wedding and the celebration."

"You're very kind, Mr. Calvin," Flavia said.

"Afterward, we won't stay too long in the city," Barnabas said. "We'll head north, where the slave catchers won't go."

"George Todd is gone," Calvin replied. "He's no longer a threat. You'll have documents proving that Flavia's a free woman."

"That won't be enough. Not to rest easy. There are stories of freed men and women kidnapped off the streets of New York and sold into slavery, taken to Virginia or the Carolinas."

"That's quite uncommon. I can't deny that it's happened a time or two, but it's very rare."

Barnabas wasn't persuaded. "Rare or not, I'd never risk it. I've seen how men look at her. She'll be safe in New Hampshire or Vermont. The farming isn't easy there, but bounty hunters don't go that far north."

"There's truth to that," Calvin said. "My family is from Boston, you know. If you will allow me to assist, I have friends who could be of service."

"Thank you, Mr. Calvin," Flavia said. "I will rest easier knowing that we can look to you for help. You have done so much for us already. To buy my freedom, and Cicero's. We can never thank you enough."

"No man or woman should ever be held in bondage," Calvin responded. "I understood that before, but with my head. Now I do with my heart."

* * *

They reached Philadelphia late in the day, and Calvin found lodging for them in an inn in the center of the city, on Main Street. The weather had been relatively mild for January, so he decided they would take the packet boat to New York. He hated the idea of being cooped up in a coach for two days, and so he arranged passage on the packet leaving that next morning.

After a hasty breakfast of salted bacon, hominy, and boiled eggs they set out for the waterfront. Rachel and Naomi were entranced by Water Street, which ran along the Delaware, and was crowded with sailors, teamsters, travelers, and vendors, all dodging the numerous carts, drays, and wagons. Calvin kept them close as they walked past the taverns and grog shops, and he saw that Barnabas had Flavia's hand firmly in his grasp.

The trip aboard the packet proved to be a swift one—down the Schuylkill River, around Cape May, and then up the New Jersey coast, past Sandy Hook, into New York harbor. As they approached Manhattan, Calvin saw that most of the city's trees were bare, branches naked and stark. They had been full of leaves the last time he had seen New York. During his extended absence, early fall had turned into deep winter.

Calvin stood by Rachel and Naomi and pointed out the familiar landmarks of New York—the spire of Trinity Church, the cluster of buildings around Federal Hall and Wall Street, the Battery at the tip of the island.

At Calvin's request, the captain of the packet had let Cicero stand by the helm and observe as they entered the harbor. It would be a good introduction to seamanship for Cicero, and if he was interested, Tarkington & Scott was always looking for seamen.

In the distance, he could just make out the forest of masts of the seagoing vessels docked along the East River, where the *Freedom* was being made ready for its March voyage to Canton. Calvin wondered when he might next go to sea. It had been more than a year, and he missed the sensation of being under sail, of the wind bearing the ship onward toward the seemingly infinite horizon, and beyond.

* * *

It took less time to reach Greenwich Street from the dock on the Hudson than Calvin had expected, and the sight of the familiar neighborhood brought sudden tears to his eyes. Embarrassed, he turned his head and rubbed his cheeks with his glove.

He had the carriage driver stop in front of his house, and bounded up the steps, eager to see Katharine, eager to resume his interrupted life. He knocked on the door impatiently several times before it was opened by a chubby red-cheeked woman.

"And who might you be?" he asked, surprised.

"Mrs. Tabitha Hopkins. Have you come to call on Mrs. Tarkington?"

"In a manner of speaking. I'm Calvin Tarkington, her husband."

"Beg pardon, sir. I didn't know."

A moment later, Katharine appeared in the foyer. "Thank God," she said. "You're alive and well."

She rushed into his arms, they embraced, and then he stepped back in surprise. "You're with child?"

"I am. I sent word by letter, but it must not have reached you. You shall be a father in the spring. Soon enough."

"Wonderful," he said. He took her into his arms again. "No need to cry, Katharine. I'm here."

"I'm sorry for the surprises. Tabitha keeps house for us. You know her husband, Arnold Hopkins. They have been of great help in your absence."

"You have no need to apologize. I didn't expect the world to stand still in my absence. And Arnold's a good man."

Calvin let go of her, and looked over his shoulder where Rachel, Naomi,

Barnabas, Flavia, and Cicero waited by the carriage. "I have my own surprises," he said. "We have guests, my dear. Perhaps Mrs. Hopkins can find something for them to eat, and I'll make the introductions."

* * *

The rest of the day was spent getting their guests settled. Calvin and Katharine had little time private together as she and Tabitha stayed busy around the house. Calvin had quickly told Katharine about Judah's death, and encouraged her to pay special attention to Rachel and Naomi.

Calvin dispatched Arnold Hopkins with messages to Richard Varick, Jean Laurent, and Livingston Rhodes announcing his return to New York. Calvin asked to see Varick in his law offices so that he could prepare the proper papers for the immediate manumission of two slaves. Calvin grinned as he penned the note—he imagined that Varick would find his request surprising and intriguing.

After an early supper, with their guests in their respective rooms, Calvin and Katharine could finally talk alone in their bedroom.

"I worried so when Christmas came and went, and you hadn't returned," Katharine said. She kissed Calvin on his lips. "I was so eager to tell you about our baby."

"A wonderful surprise," he said. "A ray of light after a very dark time."

"Judah's death?"

"More than Judah. There were others who died. There's a struggle on the frontier, between those defending slavery and those who wish to see bondage ended. Do you remember the first day we met, when you challenged me about slavery? I told you I opposed it, but other than donations to the Manumission Society I did nothing. That will change. I've had my eyes opened. I'm resolved to use whatever influence I have to end slavery in New York. If I could, I would end it everywhere."

"That may not sit well with some of those Tarkington & Scott does business with. Southern merchants."

"I'll not trim my sails on this, Katharine," he said. "I've seen too much."

"There is something I must tell you," she said.

"Must you?" he asked and kissed her gently. "That sounds so serious."

"It is serious. I've been worried about telling you this, and now you're here, and I can't delay a moment longer. Calvin, I lied to you, and to everyone, when I first came to New York. I misrepresented myself. I was never Sean Daly's wife. We lived together, but we never married. Not in a church. Not by any official."

Calvin was silent for a long moment, taking in what she had said. "Why have you waited to tell me until now?"

"I should have told you when you proposed to me. I was weak and afraid that I might lose you."

"You have not answered my question. Why tell me now?"

"When you were away, something happened—my past caught up to me. A man Sean and I knew in Dublin arrived in New York. When he learned of our marriage, he threatened to expose me." She told him about Devlin Phelan and how at first she had thought a donation to the cause of the United Irishman might satisfy him, and how she eventually turned to Livingston for assistance.

"He blackmailed you?" Calvin's jaw was set.

"He did."

"Why did you pay him anything?"

"I was ashamed. I was afraid that he would tell your friends and that they would look down on me, and that you would no longer trust me. I worried that you might leave me."

"Where is this man, Phelan, the blackmailer?"

"Somewhere at sea." She told him of Livingston's scheme, and how Phelan had "volunteered" for duty aboard the *Argos*.

"Livingston knows of this, and Captain Cushman, and Mr. Billington, his second mate?" Calvin shook his head. "Why not print the entire sordid story in the newspapers?"

"The *Argos* has sailed for the East Indies," she said. "Phelan will never return to New York. Livingston says Captain Cushman and Mr. Billington are sworn to secrecy."

"Three can keep a secret, if two of them are dead," Calvin said sourly. "Have you told me all?"

"I have," she said. "There's nothing more of import to tell."

"Nothing more about this man Phelan?"

"Nothing," she said, coloring. "Do you insinuate something?"

"I insinuate nothing, but I return home to learn that my wife has been blackmailed about her past, a past I know nothing about. All I know is what she imparts to me."

"Ask Livingston. He can corroborate what I've said."

"I've no wish to discuss this squalid episode with anyone."

"Squalid? I've done nothing to dishonor you. Do you seek a quarrel?"

"It's far from the homecoming that I had anticipated."

"And far from the reception I would expect from my husband. I tell you that I'm with child, and you don't ask about how I'm feeling, or what it's been like to be alone. You're too consumed with questioning me like you're a magistrate and I'm in the witness box."

"I'll end your cross-examination, then," he said. "I'll be in the library, catching up on correspondence. It's best that we discuss this at a later time. I don't wish to say something that I would regret later."

"Do you forgive me, Calvin? Or is that something to discuss later? I know what you are thinking, that Sarah would never have disappointed you. Perfect Sarah. I'll never live up to that paragon of virtue."

"Don't you dare speak of her in that way."

"So I'm not to speak of the ghosts in this house? Then I'll speak of myself, if that's permitted. I'm no saint, Calvin. I've made mistakes. I'm flawed. I will disappoint you again, I'm sure. You must decide if you can live with those imperfections. Or not."

TWENTY-FOUR

In the morning, Katharine greeted Calvin politely but coldly when he arrived in the kitchen for an early breakfast. He had slept poorly, sitting upright in the library's most comfortable chair. Tabitha served him a breakfast of eggs and bread, while Katharine avoided his eyes and made no attempt at conversation.

It had been their first serious quarrel, and Calvin was ashamed that he had lost his temper with her. He thought, ruefully, of Dr. Franklin's advice: "Keep your eyes wide open before marriage, half shut afterward." He knew he had been too hard on her, but he had been angry, hurt, unprepared for what she had revealed.

She had resented him asking her pointed questions about Devlin Phelan, but what did she expect of Calvin? Under the circumstances, what man wouldn't want to know more about a stranger from her past, a blackmailer? Perhaps he should have stayed silent and not pressed her. He didn't believe she was hiding anything of importance, but he wanted to know more. Wasn't he owed that?

At the same time, Calvin was angry with himself. Despite years of studying the Stoics, he had failed to remain calm and to govern his emotions. What did that suggest? He was not proud of his lack of control.

He left the house after breakfast with Barnabas, Flavia, and Cicero and went directly to Richard Varick's law office. There, a surprised Varick drew up the papers to free Cicero and Flavia—or Faith as she was now calling herself. Calvin signed the manumission documents with a flourish, and promised Varick that he would return later for further conversation. At lunch at a nearby tavern, Flavia read out loud the few brief sentences on her papers, and then did the same for an excited Cicero.

Calvin spent the remainder of the day at Water Street, meeting with Jean Laurent and Seth Elias. He worked late, and after a cold supper, served by Tabitha, he returned to the library. He stayed there after Katharine and the rest of the household had gone to bed, reading by candlelight deep into the night. The library's small fireplace provided enough warmth that he could sit in relative comfort. He fell asleep in his chair and awoke with a stiff neck at two o'clock.

When he came to bed, he found Katharine was awake. "Where have you been?" she asked.

"I fell asleep in the library," he said.

"This must not go on. I know that I've greatly disappointed you. I had hoped that you would forgive me."

"I've forgiven you."

"Have you? Is that so, Calvin? Then why did you avoid me all day? Your first day back, and you're not here for lunch or for dinner. I made excuses to *your* guests."

"I didn't feel particularly welcome this morning at breakfast. I return home to learn how little I know about my wife, and she responds with anger when I ask a few questions."

"How little you know? I've told you all that is important." She rolled over and turned her back on him. "I had thought that you would understand. I was mistaken. When I'm mistaken, I admit it. You seem incapable of that. Your pride stands in the way, Calvin Tarkington. Must you always be right?"

"Have I misused you in any way?" he asked. "If I have been distant, it's been with good cause."

"Good cause." She turned to face him, and in the dim light, he could see that her mouth was set in a firm line. "As long as you believe that, we have little of value to say to each other."

"As you would have it, then," he said, but he lay awake for most of the rest of the night.

* * *

Over the next few days, Calvin threw himself into his work. He and Katharine didn't quarrel again, but neither of them initiated a conversation of any length. More than once Calvin started to say something, but then changed his mind and remained silent.

Once Calvin had caught up with the business of Tarkington & Scott, he turned to the question of New York's laws on slavery. He called upon Alexander Hamilton to discuss the prospects of a bill banning slavery coming before the Assembly. Hamilton and Alexander Tarkington had both been on General Washington's staff, and while they had never been close, Calvin had been well received by the man nicknamed the Little Lion. At Hamilton's urging, Calvin composed and sent letters to the assemblymen he knew encouraging the consideration of the legislation.

When he visited Richard Varick at City Hall, it was clear that word of Calvin's efforts on behalf of abolition had spread, for it was the first topic Varick broached.

"You've surprised me, Calvin. In the past, you steered well clear of political disputes. Why this sudden interest in the welfare of the Negroes?"

"I've had my eyes opened. Better late than never. Ending bondage is a cause worthy of any man's support. Unlike you and my brother, I did not fight in the war for our independence. Now I have a chance to speak for liberty, and I won't shy from my duty."

"I question the wisdom of pressing for immediate abolition," Varick replied "It will stiffen the resistance by the Dutch farmers with slaves. Gradual emancipation allows owners to recoup their investment. You're a merchant. You can't expect them to take a loss."

"If need be, some modest compensation to the owners."

"What civil rights will these newly freed men have? Certainly not to vote." Varick shook his head. "We have enough common men already, too many levelers. Mr. Jefferson is counting on them for the election this fall." He looked directly at Calvin. "They want to turn me out as Mayor, you know, the Tammany crowd at Martling's."

"So I have heard. A shame, because you've done much for the betterment of the city." Calvin believed Varick had been a fine mayor, although he did think that twelve years in office was too long for any one public official. "On the question of slavery, if we don't redress this evil soon, there will come a day of judgment."

"It was a mistake to bring them here from Africa. They don't belong here. Haven't we had enough trouble with the Irish?" Varick hesitated and then coughed in embarrassment—he must have remembered that Katharine was from Dublin. "Not all the Irish, of course. No offense intended."

"There are thousands of slaves born in this country. They're Americans."

"Are they? I'd prefer to see them freed and returned to Africa. Resettled."

"And Faith, the young woman you met the other day? Should she leave the only home she's ever known?"

"Such an emigration would be voluntary, not forced."

"We disagree on this, Richard. A freed man or woman should be welcomed as a citizen. No different from you or I."

"They may be citizens in the eyes of the law," Varick said with a sad smile. "They will never be equal to you or to me. To suggest otherwise is folly. Perhaps well-intentioned, but folly nonetheless."

* * *

Livingston Rhodes had sent a message asking to meet at Tontine's Coffee House at two o'clock, and Calvin arrived early at the popular gathering spot on the corner of Wall Street and Water Street. It was a busy place, filled with brokers, merchants, traders, and underwriters, and he counted himself fortunate in finding an open table.

Livingston was five minutes late. He waited until after their coffee had been served before he spoke. "I stopped by Greenwich Street on Saturday, but you were not there."

"I was with Mr. Elias, inspecting repairs to some of the *Freedom*'s sails."

"Katharine did not know your whereabouts. I found that passing strange. From what I gathered, you have been working late since your return. Is that wise? To neglect her and your guests?"

Calvin flushed. "Have I been neglectful? Is any of this your business, Livingston?"

"She did not appear to be happy."

"I won't have you prying into my personal affairs. You strain the bonds of friendship. And I'm dismayed that Katharine would discuss this with you."

Calvin fought back his anger. Katharine had said nothing about Livingston's visit. What else did she keep from him? He knew that he was being unreasonable—they were hardly speaking—but it irritated him.

"She revealed nothing," Livingston said. "I found her sad, and elusive. Not what I would have expected. And what sort of a friend would I be if, observing her in distress, I remained silent?"

"Did I ask for you to involve yourself?"

"No, you did not. Yet I know you, and how stubborn you can be. Katharine is just as stubborn."

"It's not your place to meddle."

"Perhaps not. But I know you, Calvin. Is it a question of pride? Are you angry that she didn't tell you the truth about her relationship with Sean Daly? That she wasn't the virtuous widow?"

"She lied to me," he said flatly. "She could have told me. It wouldn't have altered my feelings for her."

Livingston snorted. "How could she be sure of that? She fell in love with you, Calvin, and she didn't want to lose you. Can you blame her for that? She's human, not some classical paragon of virtue. We all shave the truth now and then, do we not? Her motives for doing so must be seen in the proper light."

"As I said, I don't care that she hadn't married Sean Daly. You must know that."

"Do I? You act as if it did matter. As if she set out to deceive you."

"Nonsense."

"Would Katharine agree that it was nonsense? She's a fine woman. A courageous woman. She's to be the mother of your child, Calvin. Isn't it time that you swallowed your pride and sought *her* forgiveness?"

"I've listened to what you have to say," Calvin said. "I must warn you that I resent your intrusion into my private affairs. If you value our friendship, I would advise you never to raise this subject again. Do you understand me?"

"I understand you," Livingston said, his cheeks red with anger. "I understand you all too well."

"It's best if I leave now," Calvin said. "Before I say something more in anger that I will long regret."

* * *

Calvin pushed his way through the crowd at the front of Tontine's. When he reached the street, he stopped, still angry. He had never quarreled so violently with Livingston before.

He set off walking, hoping to cool down. He followed Wall Street past the Bank of New York and City Hall before reaching Trinity Church and heading north up Broad Way. He realized that he was walking toward Greenwich Street and home. A light snow had begun to fall, and the light was starting to fade.

He was troubled by what Livingston had said about Katharine and her unhappiness. Calvin knew that his friend was right—he owed her an apology. He had let his anger and disappointment get the better of him, and he had not treated her as he should have. She had kept the truth from him, but he understood why, and it didn't alter his feelings for her.

When Calvin reached the stretch of Greenwich Street by his house, he hesitated, unsure of how she would receive him. From inside, he heard music—the sound of someone playing the spinet. He entered the house and crossed through the foyer, and took the stairs two-at-a-time to the second floor. The door to the third bedroom was closed. He slowly opened it to find Katharine seated at the spinet. Calvin recognized the sonata she was playing as one that Sarah had favored.

Katharine kept playing, unaware that Calvin had come into the room. The candlelight caught her auburn hair, and there was a look on her face that Calvin could only describe as serene. He must have moved slightly, startling her, for she stopped abruptly, and looked over at him.

"Calvin," she said. "You're back early."

"That I am." He paused. "Your playing is lovely. Please continue."

She shook her head. "I shouldn't have taken the liberty. The spinet. Not without your permission."

"Nonsense. You're my wife." He moved closer to her. "Twice in my life, Livingston Rhodes has done me a great service. The first time he made me realize that I couldn't bear the thought of losing you, and that I loved you. And now, today, he has helped me see that I have been overly prideful. The past is the past. We only have the days ahead, and I want to spend them with you, Katharine. Will you forgive me?"

Her hands, now resting on her lap, trembled slightly. He reached over and took them in his hands and tears filled her eyes. "I can forgive you, Calvin, but will that be enough?"

"It will be more than enough," he said. "Please play for me."

"Only if you will sit next to me and turn the pages. I scarcely know this music."

"I want nothing more than a place by your side," he said. "A place where I hope I will always belong."

EPILOGUE

New York, January 2, 1800

Calvin welcomed the second day of the new century by joining Livingston Rhodes for lunch at No. 54 Pearl Street, Fraunces Tavern. It had become a tradition for the two to meet that day over grilled chops, pot pies, and tankards of ale, with the restaurant's famous syllabub for dessert. Fraunces held many fond memories for Calvin, from attending a dinner with his brother Alexander to honor General Washington to celebrating his marriage to Katharine.

"How is it with your household, now?" Rhodes asked with a smile once they had been seated at the table Calvin had reserved. "Cramped, I'd wager. Katharine and the twins, and Mrs. Gomez and her daughter, and the Hopkins as your servants. Two years ago you were rattling around alone in that grand house, and now I imagine that it's bursting at the seams."

"Mine is a peaceable kingdom," Calvin replied. "Despite the multitudes, I can report that harmony reigns at Greenwich Street. Tommy and Liza can be a handful, of course, so it's a benefit to have other women in the house. It makes it easier for Katharine to manage the twins. And Naomi Gomez is an adorable little girl, quite well mannered and sweet-tempered."

"I applaud your generosity in sheltering Judah's family."

"I deserve no praise. Judah was a good friend. He would have done the same for me were the circumstances reversed."

"You're too modest, Calvin. Few men would agree to take on that added responsibility. It was not your only good deed of the year. Your support of the manumission legislation was admirable. I believe that because you've held yourself aloof from politics in the past, you were quite persuasive on behalf of the bill. Of course, there were rumors that you'd become a Quaker—opposing slavery, refusing to trade in opium, all sorts of radical positions."

Calvin laughed at the thought. "I'm not dressed in black from head-to-toe, not yet. Nor will I call you, 'thee.' Shouldn't it be possible to reject profiting from the misery of our fellow humans without joining the Society of Friends?" He frowned. "In truth, the act should have gone further, and fully abolished slavery in New York once and for all. This gradual approach leaves too many in bondage."

"You know I agree with you, but it was not a simple proposition. I'd wager that half the households of means in New York have held slaves at some point. The Governor still owns a few slaves himself. There hasn't been support for immediate abolition."

"La Rochefoucauld was correct that hypocrisy is the tribute vice pays to virtue. Governor Jay knows full well slavery is wrong, and to his credit, he's tried to end it. I do understand the appeal of a gradual approach—it protects the investment of the slave owner. I once supported it. Now I'm embarrassed that I accepted the status quo for too long, excused the practice. It's an evil that must be ended. I had my eyes opened in the Northwest Territory. I've seen the violence that's necessary to keep those enslaved in bondage. They deserve liberty no less than we do."

"I believe that you came back from the frontier a changed man, at least on this question. Do you have any desire to return there?"

Calvin shook his head. "It has a wild beauty, but I prefer living by the sea. In any event, I'll not stray far from Greenwich Street for the foreseeable future. Not until Tommy and Liza are much older."

"Ah, the world traveler discovers the joys of domestic life." Livingston paused as the waiter approached them with a platter of grilled lamb chops. "What of your frontiersman friend, Barnabas? What news of him?"

"I received a letter from him just before Christmas. He and Faith live on a small farm outside Stockbridge. In fact, I brought his letter with me because I wanted to share some of it with you."

Calvin unfolded the letter and began reading it aloud:

We know that this first winter in Massachusetts may be a hard one, but we will be together, and that alone will sustain us. Faith sends her best to you and Katharine and to Rachel and Naomi. She has diligently applied herself to her reading and writing, and I trust that by this time next year she will compose her own letter to send to you. She worries about Cicero being at sea, but I have reassured her that Seth Elias is a prudent and skilled captain.

Thank you for your offer of employment with Tarkington & Scott in New York, yet I must again decline. We could never live in a state that allowed slavery in any form.

Calvin turned to his friend. "I certainly want Tommy and Liza to grow up in a country without this abominable practice."

"That day will come. Liberty for all. What we fought our revolution for."

As they ate lunch, they talked of events large and small, of whether the fall elections would favor Adams or Jefferson; of the news from Europe, where Napoleon had overthrown the Directory and been named First Consul of France; and the reports from China that the new Emperor Chia-ch'ing had graciously allowed the corrupt chief minister Ho-shen to take his own life rather than face execution for his many crimes.

After they had finished dessert, Calvin pushed back in his chair, and ran his hand through his hair. "There is something I wish to say to you, Livingston. I should have spoken of this much sooner. I owe you both thanks and an apology. First, the thanks—I'm deeply grateful for your assistance with ridding us of Devlin Phelan. An elegant, and just, resolution. And then, my apology. Last winter when you broached your concerns about Katharine's happiness, I spoke to you sharply. I was wrong to scold you then, just as I was wrong in my treatment of Katharine. You acted as a true friend should. I'm sorry, old friend."

"Apology accepted, although I'm not so ancient as to deserve the epithet of 'old.'" Livingston grinned. "Is there anything more precious than friendship? Friendship and love. They are what make us fully human. Do you recall Mr. Shakespeare's seventy-third sonnet? 'Love that well which thou must leave ere long.' He buried a young son, lost his sister to the Black Death, and his friend Christopher Marlowe to a tavern brawl. He spoke from bitter experience."

Calvin thought about the too-soon departed in his life—Alexander, Sarah, Eldedei, Judah. They had all died well before their three score years and ten promised by the Psalmist. There was no denying the fragility of human existence, nor the apparent randomness of when and how it might end for any one person—a sudden squall at sea, or a tumble from a skittish horse, or an unexpected illness.

He had cheated death enough times himself to know how close a thing it could be. What was there to do, other than to make the most of every day?

"A fine New Year's resolution," Calvin said. "To love well what we must lose someday. A resolution I shall strive to keep."

AUTHOR'S NOTE

By the close of the eighteenth century, demands for "the rights of man" were met with stiff resistance from the established order.

In Ireland, the British had moved vigorously against the Irish independence movement, harshly putting down the rising of 1798. The leader of the United Irishmen, Theobald Wolfe Tone, was captured and executed in late 1799.

In the United States, Northern abolitionists set the stage for the eventual eradication of slavery in New York. In 1799, the work of the New York Manumission Society was rewarded by the passage of "An Act for the Gradual Abolition of Slavery." The law freed all children born to slave women after July 4, 1799, once they reached the age of 25 (females) and 28 (males). However, existing slaves remained in bondage for life. The law remained silent on the legal and civil rights of freed slaves. It was not until the early 1830s that slavery was totally banned in the Empire State.

Much of the impetus for the early abolitionist movement was religious. Many of the members of the New York Manumission Society (the "New-York Society for Promoting the Manumission of Slaves, and Protecting Such of Them as Have Been, or May be Liberated") were Quakers. Pennsylvania moved sooner to end slavery than New York, in part because of the influence of the Society of Friends.

While slavery was being curtailed or extinguished in the North, it spread from the South to the Old Southwest. The invention of the cotton gin, and a growing European market for cotton, spurred the spread of slavery. The election of Thomas Jefferson in 1800 reflected a shift in federal power to the Republicans and the South. Southern Senators and

Congressmen agitated for the extension of slavery into the Mississippi Territory. Missouri entered the Union as a slave state, as did Louisiana.

What might have happened if American elites had responded to their better angels, and slavery had been outlawed in the U.S. as it had been by France in 1794, Spain (1811), and Great Britain (1834)? Would the emerging nation's economic growth have been stunted or slowed without slave labor? Or would the Southwest have been farmed by free men and women?

In the end, it would take a civil war that cost some 750,000 lives for the United States to alter course. We live with the sad legacy of slavery today and its impact on the African-American community. It has been only fifty years since the dismantling of Jim Crow segregation in the American South, and lingering racism stands in the way of a society where all might be treated as equals.

* * *

There has been a renewed academic focus on slavery in eighteenth century America, and I profited from the fresh research and insights offered by historians. Two helpful works were *The Slave's Cause: A History of Abolition* by Manisha Sinha and *The Transformation of American Abolitionism: Fighting Slavery in the Early Republic* by Richard S. Newman.

For a more comprehensive history of slavery, I found Edward E. Baptist's *The Half Has Never Been Told: Slavery and the Making of American Capitalism* a deeply researched and elegantly written narrative, although I found his arguments for the centrality of slavery in America's nineteenth century economy somewhat overstated.

For background on the struggle for Irish independence, I consulted Thomas Pakenham's *The Year of Liberty: The Great Irish Rebellion of 1798*.

The passages from Epictetus are from *The Enchiridion*, translated by Thomas W. Higginson (The Liberal Arts Press, 1948).

I would like to thank those at the Kentucky Long Rifle Foundation, the Lexington Public Library, and the Library of Congress who helped me in pinning down details of frontier life in the 1790s.

* * *

I owe my interest in American history to my father, Stephen Carver Flanders, who encouraged his children to read about the past, and took us to national parks and battlegrounds on summer vacations. He made history come to life.

Like many of my generation, I grew up with stories of the frontier, of Davy Crockett, and of Daniel Boone. (Later in life, I spent some time with Fess Parker, who played those iconic characters on television and movies, and found him to be warm and engaging).

Once again, I'm indebted to Clayton Flanders, Stephen Flanders, and Glenn Speer, who read drafts of the novel and offered helpful insights. Glenn's deep knowledge of American history proved especially valuable.

Any errors of historical fact or flaws in interpretation found in *The Northwest Country* are mine alone.

Finally, I'd like to thank my loved ones for their support, understanding, and patience as I fashioned this story.

ABOUT THE AUTHOR

Jefferson Flanders has been a sportswriter, newspaper columnist, editor, and publishing executive. He is the author of *Café Carolina and Other Stories*, *The Girl from Recoleta and Other Stories of Love*, and of the First Trumpet Cold War trilogy of *Herald Square*, *The North Building*, and *The Hill of Three Borders*.

Visit Jefferson Flanders' author website at: www.jeffersonflanders.com.

THE TARKINGTONS

The Tarkingtons, a series of novels by Jefferson Flanders about the history of a New England family begins with *The Republic of Virtue*, and continues with *The Boston Trader*.

The Republic of Virtue (Book One)

Revolutionary France, 1793. When Calvin Tarkington, a young Boston merchant-trader, arrives in Paris on July 4th, he finds a city in turmoil, riven by quarrels between revolutionary factions and threatened by advancing Coalition armies. Calvin's brother Alexander, the family firm's representative in France, has disappeared, suspected by a powerful Jacobin official of spying for the British.

As Calvin seeks to clear his brother's name, his quest for the truth takes him from elegant townhouses to squalid gambling dens to the secret chambers of the Masonic Lodge of the Seven Sisters. Drawn into a shadowy world of intrigue and betrayal, Calvin becomes the hunted as France lurches toward the Reign of Terror.

Rich in historical detail and suspense, *The Republic of Virtue* offers a moving story of love, courage, and loyalty set in a dangerous place at a dangerous time—the darkest days of the French Revolution.

The Boston Trader (Book Two)

Imperial China. When Calvin Tarkington arrives in Peking in the winter of 1795, he becomes the first American merchant to experience the sights and sounds of this exotic Imperial capital: blue-jacketed Chinese, masked against the sweeping Northern winds, crowd outdoor markets filled with the riches of Asia; proud Manchu bannermen patrol the wide boulevards and narrow alleys; and behind the vermilion walls of the

Forbidden City, mandarins, nobles, eunuchs, and concubines serve their aging Emperor, Ch'ien-lung, the Son of Heaven.

Yet Calvin cannot enjoy this moment: he has been brought to Peking to face trial on trumped-up murder charges after witnessing the assassination of an Imperial investigator in the port of Canton, the sole city open to the foreign devil *tai-pans*, a killing that is somehow linked to the growing, but illicit, opium trade.

Calvin must prove his innocence by unmasking the real killers and their connection to the corruption, misrule, and hidden treachery threatening the very stability of the Dragon Throne. He can rely only on a Manchu general and an elderly French Jesuit astronomer for help as he confronts the powerful dark forces intent on delivering him into the hands of the Imperial executioners.

The Boston Trader tells a compelling story of deception and desire, of love and betrayal, and of courage and conviction. It paints a memorable portrait of China at a turning point in its history, as the fate of the Celestial Empire hangs in the balance.